LITTLE LEAGUE
BASEBALL
A LITTLE LEAGUE BOOK

LITTLE LEAGUE®
PLAY BALL!

MATT CHRISTOPHER

Ⓛ Ⓑ
Little, Brown and Company
New York Boston

Little, Brown and Company

Hachette Book Group
1290 Avenue of the Americas, New York, NY 10104
Visit our website at www.lb-kids.com
www.mattchristopher.com

Little, Brown and Company is a division of Hachette Book Group, Inc.
The Little, Brown name and logo are trademarks of Hachette Book Group, Inc.

The publisher is not responsible for websites (or their content)
that are not owned by the publisher.

First Paperback Edition: September 2013
Originally published in hardcover in March 2013 by Little, Brown and Company

Matt Christopher® is a registered trademark of Matt Christopher Royalties, Inc.

Little League Baseball, Little League, the medallion and the keystone are registered trademarks and service marks belonging exclusively to Little League Baseball, Incorporated.

© 2013 Little League Baseball, Incorporated. All Rights Reserved.

Text written by Stephanie True Peters

Library of Congress Cataloging-in-Publication Data

Christopher, Matt.
Play ball! / by Matt Christopher.—1st ed.
p. cm.—(Little league)
Summary: "Eleven-year-old cousins who are closer than most brothers, catcher Liam McGrath and pitcher Carter Jones grew up playing baseball together. Now, their team is on the verge of winning the greatest championship of all: the Little League Baseball World Series. To reach the title match, however, they must first beat their number one rivals from Southern California. Little do they know that the game will prove to be just the first challenge they'll face on their road to the championships"—Provided by publisher.
ISBN 978-0-316-21994-5 (hc)/ ISBN 978-0-316-19975-9 (pb)
[1. Baseball—Fiction. 2. Cousins—Fiction.] I. Title.
PZ7.C458Pl 2013
[Fic]—dc23
2012028753

10 9 8 7 6

RRD-C

Printed in the United States of America

The Little League® Pledge

I trust in God

I love my country

And will respect its laws

I will play fair

And strive to win

But win or lose

I will always do my best

CHAPTER ONE

Carter Jones stood on the pitcher's mound of the Howard J. Lamade Stadium near Williamsport, Pennsylvania. The late afternoon sun beat down on the back of his neck. A trickle of sweat inched its way through his sandy hair to his temple. He ignored it, just as he ignored the throngs of spectators cheering from the stands and blanketing the famous hillside viewing area beyond the outfield fences.

He'd worked far too hard to let a little sweat and noise distract him from winning the most important game of his baseball career.

The most important game so far, the eleven-year-old southpaw amended silently.

The loudspeakers crackled. "We're at the top of the sixth and final inning of the match between Mid-Atlantic and Great Lakes," the announcer reminded the crowd. "Mid-Atlantic is up five to four. Great Lakes is at bat. Two outs, one strike, no runners on base."

As the words boomed through the park, Carter locked eyes with his catcher, Liam McGrath. Liam flashed him a quick thumbs-up.

Carter took a deep breath in through his nose and let it out slowly through his mouth. Then he set his left foot against the rubber, leaned in, and stared down at the batter.

Behind the plate, Liam shifted in his crouch and raised his mitt. The umpire bent forward, ready to make the call. Carter twirled the baseball behind his back. Once, twice around it went, until his fingertips found the seam. Then he went into his windup, reared back, and threw.

The ball flew on a line. The batter swung.

Thud!

"Steeee-rike!" the umpire bellowed.

The crowd roared like thunder. Liam stood up and hurled the ball back to Carter. Carter nabbed it, his face a mask of calm concentration.

But inside, his heart was pounding.

Mid-Atlantic was now just one strike away from victory. If the team got the win, it would move on to the U.S. Championship, where it would face the team from the West. And the winner of that game would play for the biggest prize of all—the Little League Baseball World Series title.

Carter tightened his grip on the baseball. *No pressure though*, he thought.

Truth be told, Carter couldn't quite believe he was playing in the Little League Baseball World Series. After all, it was the most celebrated of all youth sports events, and one of the most competitive, too. There were thousands of Major Little League teams throughout the world, but only sixteen made it to Williamsport for the eleven-day tournament. Those sixteen were divided evenly into two areas, with eight teams from the United States facing off in one while eight from other countries competed in the International area. The title game of the Series was a showdown between the champions.

Two months earlier, Carter never would have dreamed his All-Star team would be one of the eight from the United States. Liam, on the other hand, had predicted it the moment he saw the team's roster.

"It's stacked!" he'd crowed, his brown eyes snapping

with excitement. "Not a bad player in the bunch! I'm telling you, Carter, this is our year. We're going all the way to Williamsport!"

Carter had just smiled.

He and Liam had lived two houses away from each other since birth. Cousins who were closer than some brothers, Carter was used to Liam's wild enthusiasm and grand visions. If Carter built a snow fort, Liam built a bigger one—and then persuaded Carter to help him connect the two with a twisting maze carved in the drifts. Last summer, an unprofitable corner lemonade stand became an instant moneymaker when Liam moved their cooler of ice, juice, and cups to the busy ball field; sweaty softball players bought every last drop and the leftover ice, too. Not every scheme worked out (Carter had a jagged pink scar on his calf thanks to a fall from Liam's homemade zip-line), but that never seemed to bother Liam. He just moved on to the next adventure.

And he'd decided that this summer's adventure was getting to the Little League Baseball World Series. Carter knew better than to point out the obvious—that the road to Williamsport was a steep and incredibly difficult uphill climb. Reaching the top depended on their team playing its best each and every game, from mid-June right up through early August.

The first step on that road was beating out all the other local All-Star teams to win the District title. If they won Districts, they advanced to the next tournament, Sectionals, where they faced other District championship teams. If they were victorious in Sectionals, they played for the State title against seven other top-notch squads. And if, by some miracle, they were crowned State champs, they still had to play in the Mid-Atlantic Regional competition against the state champs from New York, New Jersey, Maryland, Delaware, and the District of Columbia! Only if they won that Regional tournament would they earn the coveted berth at the World Series.

One misstep at any point in that uphill journey and their team would tumble back to earth. Whenever Carter thought about that possibility, a worm of anxiety squirmed inside his gut.

But the team hadn't faltered. One by one, the players blew their rivals out of the water. After each win, Liam turned to Carter and said, "Admit I was right. We're going all the way."

Carter wanted to believe it was possible. But the worm of anxiety twisting inside him reminded him that the higher they climbed, the farther they had to fall. That fall would be much more painful if he attached hope to it.

So in reply, he simply said, "We're one step closer."

Even now, when they were just one out, just one single strike, away from reaching the Bracket Championship round, Carter tamped down his rising hopes and replaced them with one thought.

Focus.

He took another deep breath, turned back toward home plate, and waited for Liam's signal. His first pitch had been waist-high and to the outside corner. The batter had reached for it and missed. The pitch he'd just thrown had been to the exact same spot and yielded the same result. Would Coach Harrison send in the signal for the same pitch again?

He didn't. Instead, Liam flashed him the sign for a changeup.

Carter nodded, wound up, and threw. The moment the ball left his hand, he wished it back.

The ball dipped just ahead of the plate. The batter swung from his ankles. The bat connected with the ball. And then the ball disappeared into the blue sky.

CHAPTER
TWO

*P*ow!

Liam leaped to his feet and tore off his mask. The batter had hit Carter's pitch, but it wasn't a clean blast to the outfield. No, that ball was shooting straight up like a rocket ship—and Liam needed to be directly under it when it came back to Earth!

His brown eyes locked onto their target. He lifted his glove. It was a make-or-break moment. Make the catch, and the game was theirs. Miss it, and he'd break the hearts of his teammates, not to mention the thousands of fans who'd traveled to see their local team in action.

Liam's and Carter's families were among those fans.

Liam knew exactly where they were sitting. Before the game, they had unfurled a huge banner that read "Mid-Atlantic All the Way!"

The banner had been his mother's idea. "We'll paint the words in neon colors on a long bolt of fabric," she declared, fanning her hands out to diagram a headline in the air. "The Mid-Atlantic fans will love it!"

"Unless it's in front of them and blocking their view of the field," Carter's mother pointed out.

Her sister waved her objection away. "Then we'll take it up to the hill and invite everyone to gather under it! Imagine all of us cheering together, one big booming voice, as our home-state heroes play their way to the title!"

Liam, Carter, and everyone else in their families had pitched in to make the banner. Liam's older sister, Melanie, had even offered to hold one end, although she made it clear she had an ulterior motive.

"Your games are shown live on one of the big sports networks, right?" she'd said the week before the tournament. "They always pan around the crowd, looking for stuff like this banner. When that camera lands on me, it could be my big break."

While Liam dreamed of one day playing professional baseball, Melanie longed to make it in show business. She took every dance, voice, and acting class their small town had to offer, performed in local theater productions, and spent hours in front of the mirror perfecting her appearance. Liam's mother encouraged her every step of the way, and for all Liam knew, his sister was chock-full of talent. But living in the boondocks of Pennsylvania limited her chances of ever being "discovered"—as she complained to their parents at every opportunity. She'd once thought that New York City was where she should be, but a two-week family vacation to California the summer before had changed that. Now living near Los Angeles was all she could talk about.

For Liam's part, he couldn't imagine leaving Pennsylvania for California. He'd had a great time on their vacation. The people they'd met had been friendly and helpful, the weather had been great, and the food even better. But compared with Pennsylvania, everything about California was just so... *different.*

That afternoon, when he saw the banner on the hillside and heard the cheers from the crowd gathered by it, his heart swelled with pride and determination. Those feelings stayed with him throughout the game. They thrummed in his chest when he hit the RBI triple that gave the Mid-Atlantic players their fifth run of the game. They powered him through the long fifth inning, when Great Lakes threatened to overtake Mid-Atlantic by racking up four straight runs. And those feelings surged in his veins when Coach Harrison pulled the starting pitcher, Daniel Cho, and put Carter on the mound for the final inning instead.

His pride peaked when Carter stopped Great Lakes' rally cold. Now his determination to win took over as he tracked the ball in the air above him. It reached the top of its climb and started its descent. Liam shuffled sideways. He widened the fingers of his glove a hair more. A moment later—*Thud!* The ball landed in the pocket and stuck there!

"Yer out!" the umpire yelled.

The fans erupted, roaring, clapping, and stamping their feet. Liam leaped into the air, only to be brought back to earth when his teammates swarmed him, their screams of victory ringing throughout the ballpark.

Final score: Mid-Atlantic 5, Great Lakes 4.

Mid-Atlantic's dugout was a sea of chaos, and Liam was right in the thick of it.

"Come on, guys, cut it out!" he cried as his teammates took turns riffling his dark crew cut. "You're going to give me a bald spot!" Laughing, he dodged one more swipe of his hair and hurried to find Carter.

He spotted him sitting on the bench unlacing his cleats. He snuck up behind him and snatched off his cap.

"Hey!" Carter whirled around. "Give it back, doofus!"

Liam waved the hat over his head. "First admit I was right, dork. We're going all the way!"

Carter grinned and pushed his shaggy light brown hair behind his ears. "We're one step closer. Now give me my cap."

Instead Liam danced away, brandishing the cap like a flag and chanting, "We're going all the wa-ay! We're going all the wa-ay! Admit I'm right, admit I'm right! We're going all the wa-ay!"

He looked over his shoulder then, expecting to see Carter shaking his head or rolling his eyes. But his cousin wasn't even looking at him. He was standing stock-still and staring at the stands.

Puzzled, Liam followed Carter's gaze. He spotted a boy wearing a West team jersey and matching baseball cap.

"You know that kid?" Liam asked.

Carter started as if he'd forgotten Liam was there. "Yeah," he muttered. "He was at baseball camp with me. He's a pitcher."

The summer before, Carter had attended the prestigious Little League Baseball Camp in Williamsport.

Liam had hoped to go, too, and was bitterly disappointed when he found out that Carter's session fell right in the middle of his family's California vacation. Their mothers had tried to switch Carter's week to another, but all the other sessions were full. So when camp time rolled around, Carter went alone.

Liam looked at the boy with new interest. "Hold on a second! We're playing his team in the U.S. Championship, right?"

Carter turned away and started collecting his gear. "So?"

A tingle of excitement shot up Liam's spine. "So you spent a week playing baseball with this guy! You can give us the scoop on him! What're his weaknesses? What's his favorite pitch to throw? Can he hit? Is he—"

Carter cut him off. "All I know is that he's the biggest jerk I've ever met."

The anger in Carter's voice caught Liam off guard. Lots of kids called other people names, or bad-mouthed them behind their backs. Not Carter. In fact, Liam had heard his cousin say something like that about only one other person.

They'd been eight years old and playing catch in Carter's backyard. Suddenly, there was a squeal of tires followed by a high-pitched yelp. Carter had dashed to the front yard before Liam had even registered the sounds. Moments later, he found Carter kneeling over a small black-and-tan dog. Carter was making soothing sounds, clearly trying to calm the injured dog. He looked up at Liam with stunned disbelief that quickly turned to anger.

"He didn't even stop! That—that—*idiot* just kept driving like nothing happened! If I ever find out who that jerk was I'll—"

Liam never found out what Carter intended to do, because Carter's mother appeared at that moment. Mrs. Jones rushed the dog to the veterinarian hospital. Three days later, the dog's injuries were on the mend. Carter and Liam posted signs about having found a lost dog, but no one claimed him. So the Joneses adopted him, and Carter gave him his name: Lucky Boy.

Liam hadn't thought about the hit-and-run for a long time. But he had never forgotten Carter's fury— nor had he ever heard his cousin sound that angry again. Until now.

What did that kid from West do to make Carter dislike him so much? he wondered.

Just as he was about to ask, however, someone grabbed him from behind.

CHAPTER
THREE

Carter knew his aunt Amanda was waiting for them even before he saw her.

"I am so proud of you two I could just burst!" she cried. A midsize woman with a supersize personality, she swept Liam up in a one-armed embrace, wrapped her other arm around Carter, and then crushed them together in a huge bear hug.

"Mom, you're squishing the air out of us!" Liam protested, laughing.

"Nonsense! Carter's not complaining, are you, Carter?"

Carter's mother saved him from having to answer. A carbon copy of her older sister in looks, with the same medium brown hair and light brown eyes, Cynthia

Jones winked at him and said, "Amanda, would you mind if I congratulated my boy now?"

Mrs. McGrath gave Carter one more squeeze and then released him. As Liam's father and sister crowded around Liam—"I'm so jealous! Every camera in the stadium was on you when you made that catch!" Melanie moaned—Mrs. Jones folded Carter into her arms.

"Wow," she whispered. "You were amazing."

"Thanks, Mom," he whispered back.

"Well done, son," his father added, beaming.

"Enough with the mushy stuff," Amanda cut in. "You boys head up to the Media Center for Coach Harrison's postgame interview."

Liam struck a pose. "Do I look all right, Melanie? I'll probably get on camera again, you know!"

She yanked his cap down over his face. "There, that's perfect!"

The families left then. Carter started for the stairs that led to the concourse level of the stadium, where the Media Center was. He'd gone only one step, however, when Liam pulled him back.

"Hang on, Carter," he said. "The interview isn't for another few minutes. That's plenty of time for you to tell me what that kid from West did to make you so mad."

If anyone else had asked, Carter would have pretended he wasn't mad, just surprised to see the other boy. But he knew he'd never fool his cousin.

"You know how I said I lost my Little League Baseball Camp jersey? Well, I didn't lose it. I threw it away."

Liam raised his eyebrows in surprise. "Why? You told me camp was awesome."

"It was, for the first two days, anyway."

Carter thought he'd be homesick at camp without Liam, but he was so busy he didn't have time to be. Out of bed by seven, breakfast by seven thirty, and then two hours of intense baseball practice starting at nine. Carter worked harder and learned more about playing in those sessions than he ever had in his life. He gauged his improvement by how he played in the daily afternoon games. He wasn't a great hitter, but he made good, solid plays at his third-base position.

Liam interrupted. "It was during the third morning practice that your coach asked you to take the mound, right?"

"Right."

Thinking Mr. Cobb had him confused with someone else, Carter reminded the coach that he played third base.

"I realize that," Mr. Cobb said. "But I have a hunch

about you. Your throws are powerful, accurate, and controlled. Plus, you're left-handed. Many batters struggle when they face southpaws. If you can pitch, you could become a valuable asset to any team."

So Carter gave it a try. After a few misfires, the coach corrected his mechanics. To Carter's astonishment, his next pitch socked into the catcher's glove with a satisfying *pop*.

The coach nodded knowingly. "You definitely have potential."

Liam cut in again. "So after that practice, you got all fired up to be the best hurler in the Little League, which of course was a brilliant idea since I'd been working on becoming the best catcher. Now you and I together are like peanut butter and jelly." He kissed his fingertips. "Perfection!"

"Yeah," Carter said slowly. "Except it wasn't that practice that made me want to pitch. It was something that happened after that."

Liam gave him a long look. "That something has to do with your missing jersey and that kid from West, doesn't it?"

Carter nodded. "He's a pitcher, the best pitcher at camp, actually. We played his team that same afternoon. He pitched a great game. He hit well, too. His team probably would have won if I hadn't tagged him out at third in the last inning.

"Anyway, after the match, I told him my coach thought I had potential to be a pitcher and asked him what it was like to pitch."

The boy hadn't replied at first. He just looked Carter up and down. Finally, he shrugged and said, "There's a lot of pressure on the mound. You know, coaches, teammates, and fans all staring at you, expecting you to throw a perfect pitch every time, disappointed when you don't. Every batter looking to light you up like a Christmas tree, maybe even drill you with a line drive." He gave Carter a penetrating look. "Think you could handle that kind of stress?"

Carter shifted his gear bag to his other hand. "I—I don't know. Maybe."

The boy turned away as if he found the answer disappointing. "Well, when you're sure, come talk to me again. I'm Phillip, Phillip DiMaggio."

Carter stopped short when he heard that name. "DiMaggio?"

"Yeah."

"As in . . . *Joe* DiMaggio?"

Phillip turned back slowly. His mouth twitched. "That's right." He leaned in close and whispered, "Not everyone knows this, but my great-grandfather's name was Joe."

"Wow!" Carter breathed. He stared at the boy, taking in his wide-set dark eyes, long nose, and lanky frame. He hadn't seen it before—but now that he knew he was talking to the great-grandson of Joltin' Joe DiMaggio, the late great Yankee center fielder, he saw the family resemblance plainly!

Fingers shaking with excitement, he dug a permanent marker out of his bag. "Would you...do you think you could sign my jersey?"

"Oh, sure." Phillip thought for a moment and then with thick, bold strokes, wrote *To Carter Jones, DiMaggio's Number One Fan!* on the jersey's shoulder.

Liam broke into the story again. "Hold on," he said, frowning. "Joe DiMaggio only had one son. That son didn't have any kids of his own. So Phillip DiMaggio can't be the Yankee Clipper's great-grandson."

"No kidding," Carter said shortly. "Too bad I figured that out *after* he'd signed my shirt."

He didn't know why Phillip had tricked him into believing he was descended from Joe DiMaggio. But Phillip clearly enjoyed the prank. Now, every time he saw Carter, he shouted, "Hey, look, everyone! It's my Number One Fan! Don't believe me? Just check out his jersey!"

Carter tried his best to ignore him, but when other campers started calling him Number One Fan as well, he knew he had to do something. So he redoubled his efforts on the field, pouring every bit of energy he had into practices and soaking up everything he could learn about pitching.

His hard work paid off. His coach started him at pitcher in the final game of the session. Campers were heading home right afterward, so the stands were filled with parents. Carter had swallowed his nervousness and struck out three batters in the four innings he pitched. The icing on the cake had come after the game, when one of his teammates said, "We're going to drop the *Fan* and just call you Number One!" It felt good to hear that, and Carter realized he loved being a pitcher.

Still, he couldn't erase the embarrassment of DiMaggio's prank. So the first thing he did when he got home that afternoon was bury the jersey deep in the trash can. *I hope I never hear the name DiMaggio again!* he thought as he slammed down the lid.

"I thought that was the end of it," Carter told Liam. "But now I have to face that jerk the day after tomorrow!"

He expected his cousin to sympathize with him. But to his surprise, Liam burst out laughing.

CHAPTER
FOUR

What's so funny?"

The irritation in Carter's voice helped Liam get himself under control. "Don't you get it?"

"Get what?"

"DiMaggio did you a huge favor!"

Carter looked at him like he was crazy.

"You're not looking at the big picture," Liam explained. "Your coach tells you you've got great potential, right? DiMaggio feels threatened by you, so he points out all the bad stuff about pitching. Then he goes one step further and tries to humiliate you in front of the rest of the camp. But that plan blows up in his face. Sure, you looked like an idiot—"

"Oh, thanks!"

"—but somewhere in that pea brain of yours—"

"Thanks again!"

"—you decided that the best way to get back at DiMaggio was to become the best pitcher you could be." Liam gestured to the field in front of them. "And now look! We're playing at the Lamade Stadium in *the Little League Baseball World Series*, man! And you know what else?" he added with a mischievous twinkle in his eye.

"What?"

"We're going to go all the way! Now, come on. The press conference starts any minute."

With that, they raced up the stairs to the interview room.

"Liam, Carter, excellent!" Coach Harrison boomed when he spotted them. "I thought you were going to miss tonight's press conference." He ushered them to a table in front of the wall covered with Little League emblems.

Media coverage of the Little League Baseball World Series was intense, with games covered on television, radio, and in newspapers around the country. To Liam's eye, not all coaches seemed comfortable in front of the microphone. But Coach Harrison handled the conference like a pro.

A wiry man with thick black hair, beefy arms, and a snub nose, he kept his answers to questions short and sweet, conveying his delight in his players' victory and praising their ability to play together like a well-oiled machine.

"I know that image is overused in sports," he added, "but with these guys, it's accurate. They meshed the moment they stepped onto the field together. I couldn't ask for a better bunch of kids." Then he grinned. "Fortunately, I might not have to. Most of these guys are eleven years old. They've got another whole year in the Majors and so could all be here again next year. And if they're lucky, I'll be their coach next year, too!"

Applause and laughter followed that statement and then the conference was over.

Later that evening, Liam and Carter headed to the recreation center of the Dr. Creighton Hale International Grove. The Grove was the players' home throughout their stay in Williamsport. Four brick buildings housed four teams each, two from the United States and two from other countries. Players from the world over mingled during meals in the dining hall, but the rec center was where they really got to know one another. There, they played Ping-Pong, air hockey, and video games, swam in a huge inground pool, and watched television. They also traded collectible pins in a special area set aside for that activity.

Liam and Carter had been trading pins for a few years. Each had a decent collection; Liam kept his in a black, zippered canvas bag. Carter had a similar bag, but his was brick red. Now they carried those bags to the center, hoping to add a few unusual pins through swaps with international players. They'd only just entered the second-floor room when suddenly—

"Number One Fan!"

A figure pushed off from a wall near the door, almost as if he'd been waiting for them. Liam had seen Phillip DiMaggio only from a distance. But there was no mistaking who he was. The taunt and Carter's expression told him loud and clear.

Two other boys—teammates, Liam guessed—sidled up beside Phillip. Phillip planted his hands on his hips and repeated, "Number One Fan! I wondered when I'd run into you!"

Liam sized up the situation in a split second. DiMaggio had known Carter was playing in the Series. Somehow, he'd kept his own presence there a secret. But now, when Carter most needed to keep his focus, Phillip was doing his best to jar him. And from what Liam could see, it was working.

Well, two can play at that game, Liam thought. *You try to throw him off guard? I'll do the same to you!*

Figuring the West boys were anticipating a confrontation, he gave them the exact opposite. He stepped forward and held out his hand.

"Hi, I'm Liam McGrath!" he said cheerily. "Looks like we're playing you in the U.S. Championship."

Phillip was clearly nonplussed. He glanced at Liam's hand but didn't shake it.

After a moment, Liam pulled it back and ran his fingers through his hair, pretending he'd meant to do that all along. "So, where in California are you from? I visited relatives outside San Fernando last summer while Carter was at Baseball Cam—anyway," he interrupted himself hastily. "Yeah, San Fernando. Pretty cool area. Ever hear of it?"

One of Phillip's teammates rolled his eyes. "Are you serious? We're *from* the San Fernando area. It's only mentioned in every game write-up."

"Oh," Liam said. "So I guess you have heard of it."

Dead silence met this obvious statement.

"Right. Well, Carter and I have to get going. See you

guys on the field." Liam started to move around the boys, but then stopped short. "Oh, gee, Phil, you've got something on your shirt"—he touched a spot a few inches beneath DiMaggio's chin—"right here."

As Liam had hoped, DiMaggio glanced down. Quick as a flash, Liam jerked his finger up and pegged him in the nose. He didn't know who looked more surprised: DiMaggio, his sidekicks, or Carter.

"Ha! Made you look!" Liam burst out laughing. "I can't believe you fell for that! It's, like, the oldest trick in the book. Somehow, I expected more from you."

Before Phillip could react, Liam grabbed Carter's arm and pulled him toward the pin-trading area.

"What did you do that for?" Carter sputtered when they were out of earshot.

Liam held up his hands in mock-surrender. "Hey, I tried being friendly. All he had to do was shake my hand. He didn't, so instead he got the classic made-you-look nose bop."

Carter shook his head. "I don't know. It might not have been such a good idea to make DiMaggio mad."

"Oh, please," Liam said. "We'll play him in one game. We'll win, and then we'll never have to see him again. And in the meantime, do me a favor. If he calls you Number One Fan before the game, channel your anger into your pitching!"

Carter rolled his eyes, but Liam could see a smile starting at the edge of his lips. He pushed on.

"Listen, you and me and all the other guys on Mid-Atlantic have worked too hard to let him stop us from going all the way. Am I right? Huh? Huh?" He jabbed him a few times to emphasize his point.

Carter batted Liam's elbow away and drove into him with a shoulder, shoving him away. "You're a doofus, but you're right," he said. "So, okay, if DiMaggio tries to get in my head before the championship, I'll just block him out. You know, like I block you out when you try to be funny."

Carter spoke with confidence. Liam hoped he felt confident, too. Because if he didn't, Liam knew it would show the minute he stepped onto the mound. He knew something else, too: if his cousin buckled against West, their team could kiss the U.S. Championship and the chance to play in the World Series title game good-bye.

CHAPTER
FIVE

Two nights later, the bleachers and hillside of Lamade Stadium were once again packed to capacity. Floodlights illuminated the immaculately groomed field, music blared from the loudspeakers, and the Little League mascot, Dugout, led the crowds in enthusiastic cheers.

Those cheers grew even wilder when the two teams raced onto the diamond to warm up.

Because he lived so close to Williamsport, Carter had been to the Little League Baseball World Series a few times in the past, but always as a spectator, never a player. He tried not to think about all those people as he jogged around the outfield with his teammates.

As he drew near the West's dugout, Carter picked

up his pace. Two words ran through his head, matching his left-right footfalls.

Don't-look, don't-look, don't-look.

He looked. And immediately wished he hadn't, for staring back at him, a smile slowly widening across his face, was Phillip DiMaggio.

"Number One Fan! Find me after we win and I'll sign your jersey again!" DiMaggio called.

Laughter from the dugout chased Carter all the way to the first-base line.

So did Liam. "Remember: Channel your anger into your pitching," he murmured when he caught up.

Carter slowed to a walk, bent forward, and took a few slow breaths. "I'll try," he promised through gritted teeth.

Liam lifted a finger. "As the great Jedi Master Yoda said, 'Do, or do not. There is no try.' "

Carter was saved from responding when Coach Harrison called the team together for a pregame pep talk. "This is it, boys!" he said, bouncing on his toes. "Win today and you'll be in the World Series Championship. That's something no team from the Mid-Atlantic region has accomplished in years."

He pointed at them. "Can you do it? Yeah, you can, because you've got the talent, the drive, and something else besides!" He waited a beat and then slapped his chest and grinned broadly. "You've got me!"

As Carter joined in the laughter, he felt his tension ease a little.

The coach offered a few more words of encouragement. Then the loudspeakers whined, and the voice of the game announcer boomed forth.

"Ladies and gentlemen, welcome to the United States Championship Game of the Little League Baseball World Series between Mid-Atlantic and West!"

He paused while the spectators applauded. "There's a lot on the line today, folks, for the winner of the game goes on to face the International Champion for the World Series title! Here's today's lineup for the team from Southern California." He rattled off the roster and, again, waited for the applause to die down before introducing Carter's team.

"Mid-Atlantic won the coin toss and so plays as the home team today. That's pretty appropriate, for the squad itself is from this fine state, Pennsylvania!"

This time the applause was even louder and longer— not surprising, since the bulk of the audience came from Pennsylvania.

As his name was called, each member of Mid-Atlantic jogged onto the field until the team stood shoulder to shoulder, hands behind their backs. When the last one, right fielder Craig Ruckel, had joined the line, the announcer invited everyone to stand for the National Anthem.

Cap over his thumping heart, Carter sang along, tuning out Liam's off-key warble as best as he could. When the anthem ended, the cousins bumped fists three times for good luck.

As the home team, Mid-Atlantic was in the field first. Gloves in hand, they spread out on the diamond. Then the umpire bellowed the two words baseball fans love best:

"Play ball!"

Carter received the game ball. The gleaming white sphere fit into his left hand so perfectly, it was as though he'd been born with it there. He rotated it until he felt the seams beneath his fingers. Then he looked at Liam behind home plate. Even though he couldn't see his cousin's eyes clearly through his catcher's mask, Carter knew they were delivering him a silent message.

You can do this.

And in that moment, Carter believed he could.

The first batter stepped into the box. Carter squared his shoulders, placed his left foot on the rubber, and leaned in for the sign.

Fastball, high and inside.

He nodded.

Even from forty-six feet away, Liam's mitt looked as big as a barn to Carter. With his glove shielding his grip on the ball—no point in advertising that he was throwing a two-seam fastball—he went through his windup, then took a powerful lunging step forward, and whipped the ball up and over his shoulder. A sharp snap of his wrist sent the ball whizzing toward Liam's glove.

Zip! Swish! Thud!

"Strike one!"

Liam had barely moved to catch the pitch. But he didn't smile when he stood up to throw the ball back to Carter. Carter didn't smile, either. It was a good, clean strike, but it was only one. If Mid-Atlantic was going to win, he had to deliver more—a *lot* more.

He did just that, at least in the first two innings. Of the six batters he faced, three were sent packing on three pitches each, all strikeouts. The other three connected, but only one West player made it to first base. He never reached second, though, because the next batter popped out into a double play. The top of the second inning ended with the West still scoreless.

As Carter trotted off the mound to the dugout, the coach called his name. "You're up to nineteen pitches,"

Coach Harrison informed him. "You know what that means."

Carter sucked in his breath and nodded.

Unlike other youth baseball organizations, Little League had strict rules about the number of times a pitcher could throw in a game. The rules were designed to prevent arm injuries.

The pitch count worked on a sliding scale and depended on the player's age. As an eleven-year-old, Carter was allowed to throw no more than eighty-five in a single game. Anywhere between sixty-six and eighty-five pitches, and he had to rest four days before he could take the mound again. If he threw between fifty-one and sixty-five, he could pitch after three days' rest. He could pitch again after two days if his count was between thirty-six and fifty, and after one day if he threw between twenty-one and thirty-five. Twenty or fewer, and the pitcher was allowed to take the mound again the next day.

The next day, in this case, was the day of the World Series Championship.

If Carter pitched just two more times today, he wouldn't be allowed to pitch in the game tomorrow. If he came out of today's game right now, however, he could take the mound for at least some of that title match. Of course, to even play in that game at all, Mid-Atlantic had to win this game.

Coach Harrison tapped his clipboard thoughtfully. Carter knew he was weighing whether to keep him in or take him out.

Liam must have known it, too, because he sat down next to Carter and whispered, "Man, I hope you stay in, because you're pitching great! And you'll still get in the game in some other position tomorrow."

After a long moment, Coach Harrison made his decision. "You're on the mound again next inning, Carter. Now get going, Liam. You're up first!"

As Liam shoved a helmet onto his head, he leaned in and whispered to Carter, "You-know-who is still in, too, don't forget."

Carter glanced at the mound. Sure enough, Phillip DiMaggio was there.

Liam grinned at Carter and then headed to the plate. His easy, rolling gait made him appear as if he were out to enjoy a Sunday stroll rather than face a steely-eyed pitcher. He hadn't had his growth spurt yet, so he was a little on the short side. There was a hint of pudge to him, too. But crammed into that small, squat package was a very efficient hitter who had taken more than one pitcher by surprise.

"I imagine I'm a spring, wound tight and ready to go," he'd once told Carter. "Hit the release button and *wham!* I uncoil and hit that pill out of the park!"

Carter had tried visualizing the same thing, but it just didn't work for him the way it did for Liam. He watched his cousin with envy, wishing he could collect hits like Liam did.

And Liam did get a hit—almost. Phillip unleashed a sizzling fastball. Liam connected, sending the sweet sound of bat meeting ball ricocheting around the stadium. But that sound was followed immediately by another.

Thud!

With catlike reflexes, Phillip DiMaggio had leaped off the mound, stuck out his glove, and caught the line drive!

CHAPTER
SIX

Liam was stunned when he saw the ball sticking out of DiMaggio's glove. "I'm—out?" he sputtered. "Unbelievable!"

"Believe it!" the catcher said gleefully. "DiMaggio's the best of the West and all of the rest!"

Still dazed, Liam trotted back to the dugout. Carter started to say something, but Liam waved him off. "No comment," he muttered.

Outfielder Charlie Murray was up next. He hit a rolling grounder between short and third that should have been an easy out. But the shortstop bobbled the pickup, giving fleet-footed Charlie just enough time to land on base.

Now it was Carter's turn to hit. Liam studied his cousin as he walked to the right side of the plate. Carter was tall and lean, just the right build for a pitcher—and just the kind of build Liam wished he himself had. Somehow, it didn't seem fair that Carter, who was two months younger, had a three-inch height advantage.

Genetics in action, he thought ruefully. Carter's father stood at six feet, two inches. He was a lefty, too, like Carter. Since his own dad was only five foot ten, Liam figured he had as much chance of reaching six feet as he did of growing wings. *Nothing I can do about it, so I might as well learn to live with it!*

He turned his attention back to the field in time to see DiMaggio release the ball.

"Too high," Liam muttered, willing Carter to let it go by.

Carter did. He let the next two go as well. He took a cut at the fourth, but missed.

Three balls, one strike. The next pitch came in at eye level, way above the strike zone.

"Ball! Take your base!" the umpire called.

Carter tossed his bat aside and jogged to first. Charlie moved from first to second. Liam cheered along with his teammates and the fans, although something about the last pitch bothered him.

He tried to figure out what it was as Ted Sandler, Mid-Atlantic's second baseman, readied himself in the batter's box. Ted was a good fielder, but statistically not very strong at the plate. It was when Ted fouled a pitch down the first-base line that Liam decided DiMaggio must know that.

He walked Carter on purpose, figuring there's a good chance that Ted will hit an easy grounder or a pop-up. Then they can go for a double play!

Ted started to go for the second pitch, only to check his swing. Unfortunately, he didn't stop in time.

"Strike two!" the umpire called.

Ted backed out of the batter's box and fussed with his helmet. It was a delay tactic, pure and simple. The grin on Phillip's face indicated he'd guessed why Ted had done it.

Ted has to swing and he's worried. If DiMaggio's studied Ted's stats, then he knows Ted doesn't hit well in a pressure situation. He's already thrown two fastballs. I bet he's going to throw a changeup now.

That was exactly the pitch DiMaggio threw. Ted connected, but misjudged the deceptive pitch. Instead of flying high and far, the ball dribbled to the left of the mound. The shortstop ran in, scooped it up, and tossed it to third. Charlie was out. The third baseman quickly relayed the ball to second. For a moment, Liam thought Carter was safe, but then the umpire jerked his thumb and cried, "Yer out!"

Double play. The inning was over.

The teams switched sides. Liam tugged his mask into position and hustled to the plate. While he waited for Carter to reach the mound, he glanced over toward the West dugout. Phillip, the West's leadoff batter for this inning, was taking a few practice cuts. It was the first chance Liam had had to really study his swing. He narrowed his eyes, trying to detect a pattern.

Does DiMaggio drop his back shoulder when he swings? If so, then Carter should aim high. Or does he—

Thud. Thud. Thud. Liam's thoughts were interrupted by a noise coming from the mound. Carter was slamming the ball into his glove, over and over again.

Uh, oh, Liam thought.

Many of his teammates had nervous habits. Charlie yanked on his shirtsleeves. Oliver Ackerman fiddled with his cap. The few who didn't have braces chomped on gum.

Carter's habit was to throw the ball into his mitt. The more nervous he was, the harder the ball socked into the glove. Right now, he was hurling the ball so hard Liam's own hand stung just watching.

Phillip was watching Carter, too. His mouth bent into a half smile.

Liam frowned. Did DiMaggio know Carter was nervous? *I bet he does,* he realized, *because I bet he saw Carter do that when they were at camp!*

He tried to signal his cousin that his motion was telegraphing his anxiety. But before he could catch his eye, the umpire cried, "Batter up!"

Phillip took one last swing, strode to the plate, and hefted the bat over his shoulder.

As Liam got into his crouch, he shot a quick glance at DiMaggio's feet. DiMaggio was in an even stance, feet parallel and toward the front of the box but back from the plate.

Fastball to the outside, Liam thought instantly. He glanced at Coach Harrison, who signaled him to give that pitch. *Let's see how good your reaction time and reach are, DiMaggio.* Liam flashed one finger followed by a tap on the inside of his right thigh.

Carter chewed on his lip and nodded. He wound up and delivered. The pitch came in fast, but was so far outside that Liam had to lunge to the right to make the catch. Phillip didn't even move.

"Ball one!"

The next pitch was another ball. Again, Phillip stood like a statue.

Liam took a moment to adjust his crouch. As he did, he made a patting motion with his bare hand. *Calm down* that motion was meant to say to Carter. He hoped Carter saw it.

Carter's third pitch was right on target—if the target had been DiMaggio's rib cage. Phillip gave a surprised yelp and sprang out of the way.

"Ball three!"

On the sidelines, Coach Harrison had clearly seen enough.

"Time!" he cried. "Liam!"

Liam knew what the coach wanted. He waited until the umpire waved his arms through the air, signaling for play to stop, and then hurried out to the mound.

"The count's three-and-oh, so he's going to let the next one go by," he reminded Carter. "You've got to throw one in the strike zone so he doesn't get a walk."

Carter thumped the ball into his glove. "But what if he swings?"

Liam put a reassuring hand on his shoulder. "So what if he does? What's the worst that can happen?"

CHAPTER
SEVEN

Carter was about to tell Liam exactly what the worst could be when the umpire ordered them to resume playing.

He's right about one thing, though, he thought as he set his foot against the rubber. *I've got to throw a strike.*

So when Liam signaled for a fastball right down the middle, that's what Carter threw.

And that's what DiMaggio hit. *Pow!*

Carter shook his head in disgust as he watched Phillip round the bases, grinning from ear to ear and hamming it up for the roaring crowd. *That's the worst that can happen, Liam.*

But if Liam was troubled by the home run, he didn't

show it. Instead, he pounded his fist into his mitt and got into his crouch as if giving up a run to the inning's leadoff hitter was nothing to worry about.

And maybe it isn't, Carter thought suddenly. *We still have four innings at bat. That's plenty of time for us to chalk up some runs of our own!*

With that thought firmly in mind, he squared his shoulders and faced the second batter. One pitch later, that batter was trudging back to the dugout, his pop fly nestled in Miguel's glove.

One out.

The third hitter hit the first pitch for a bouncing grounder that Carter scooped up and tossed to first.

Two outs.

The fourth man up brought the West players back to the top of their order. He made Carter work much harder. He nicked pitch after pitch, sending three balls foul before finally straightening one out. Luckily, shortstop Miguel Martinez was ready. He fielded the ball cleanly and sent it to first base for the final out.

"Good job, good job," Coach Harrison called, clapping loudly. He pointed to the team's third baseman, Leonard Frick. "Leo, you're up! Oliver, you're after Leo. Then we're back to the start of the lineup with Miguel and Jerry. And let's see if we can give Remy a chance at bat, too!"

After two batters, however, Remy Werner's chances of getting up didn't look good. Leo struck out on three pitches and Oliver popped out.

Miguel already had on a batting helmet. Now he chose his favorite bat, took a few swings through the air, and strode to the plate. An oversize boy with an olive complexion, Miguel liked to aim for the fences. Sometimes he reached them. This time, he got a single with a short hopper toward the hot corner. The third baseman ran in, gloved the ball, and made a strong throw to first. Fortunately for the Mid-Atlantic team, that throw wasn't in time.

Now Jerry Tuckerman, the team's first baseman, moved to the batter's box. He dug his front toe in the dirt, hefted the bat over his shoulder, and waggled his hips.

On the mound, Phillip stood still for a few beats. The brim of his cap cast a dark shadow over his face. Looking at him, Carter shivered involuntarily; for a moment, the space beneath the cap appeared to be a faceless mask, completely devoid of features and expression.

Then Phillip shifted and his expression came into clear focus: ferocity mingled with supreme confidence.

He probably practices that look in the mirror, Carter thought, *to psyche out batters.* He wondered if it worked.

Whether it was his look or his pitching, Phillip confounded Jerry at bat. Jerry was usually good for a bouncing grounder, but this time he pinged three fouls before fanning the fourth pitch.

Three outs, and another scoreless inning for Mid-Atlantic. Mid-Atlantic returned the favor, however, retiring three batters in order. It had taken a lot of work, though—fourteen pitches, by Carter's count, bringing his total number that game to forty-three.

No problem, he thought.

"Bottom of the fourth, West is up one run to none. A lineup change brings outfielder Craig Ruckel to the plate," the announcer reported. Moments later, he added, "And Ruckel is out on a caught foul ball. Next up is Liam McGrath. The team's power hitter, McGrath lined out earlier in the game thanks to a fantastic defensive effort by West's pitcher, Phillip DiMaggio. Let's see who wins in the matchup this go-around."

Carter watched his cousin approach the plate. There was nothing relaxed and easygoing about his walk this time. Everything about Liam screamed one thing: determination.

A thrill shot through Carter. He leaned forward.

"He's going to cream it!"

Carter hadn't realized he'd spoken the thought out loud until Leo, sitting next to him, said, "Man, I sure hope so! We need a hit!"

Carter stared at him. Then he leaped to his feet and cried. "So let's make some noise and let him know we're behind him one hundred percent!"

The other boys jumped up, too, and began bellowing words of encouragement.

"Go, Liam, go!"

"You're the man, Liam!"

"He's scared of you!"

"You can do it!" Carter shouted at the top of his lungs. Then he, his teammates, and everyone else in the stadium held their breath as the pitcher sent the ball screaming toward the plate.

CHAPTER
EIGHT

*Y*um.

That was the thought that flashed through Liam's mind when he saw the pitch. It looked like a tasty meatball, served up on a silver platter just for him. He swung with all his might.

Pow!

It wasn't a home run, just a good solid hit that landed deep in the pocket between left and center field. As he dropped the bat and raced toward first, Liam had a fleeting glimpse of Phillip's face. He liked what he saw there almost as much as the roars from the people in the stands. The combination spurred him on to second, where he captured the base standing up.

"Here we go, Charlie, send me home!" he cried, pounding his hands together.

But Charlie grounded out.

"Now batting, Ca-aa-arter Jones!" the announcer drawled.

Carter moved to the plate amid loud cheers and whistles. Liam added his own before settling down for whatever came next. It was a good thing he did, because what came next was a thumping line drive off Carter's bat!

The ball sizzled through the gap between first and second. Liam flew like a bullet to third.

"Go! Go! Go!" the third-base coach screamed.

Liam touched the bag, cornered sharply, and kept running. He heard the crowd gasp.

I'm going to be tagged out! Faster, feet! Faster!

And then suddenly, he was sliding into home plate, skidding past the catcher across the pointed end.

"Safe!" the umpire bellowed.

Mid-Atlantic was on the board at last!

Grinning broadly, Liam jumped up and whirled around to see where Carter was. First base? Second? Maybe even *third*?

But Carter wasn't on any base. He was running off the field. Around him, the West players were hustling to their dugout.

Liam blinked in confusion and then hurried to the bench. He caught Daniel Cho's arm. "What happened?" he demanded.

Daniel shook his head. "Carter stumbled rounding first. He was tagged out at second," he said.

"But my run!" Liam cried. "Did it count or not?"

"It did, but just barely. You touched the plate only a few seconds before Carter was tagged."

"Oh, man." Liam watched his cousin make his way back to the dugout. His head was bowed as if he were too disappointed to look anyone in the eye.

But as he stepped beneath the overhang, Carter looked up. Instead of disappointment, his eyes blazed with pure fury. "He tripped me!" he spat.

Liam's eyebrows shot up into his hair. "He who?"

"Who do you think? DiMaggio! That's who!" Carter shouted. "He covered first on my hit. When I started for second, he moved his foot right where mine was going to land!"

"You mean he kept you from reaching second? That's obstruction!" Liam cried. "Come on, we've got to let Coach Harrison know!"

The coach looked very grave when they told him what had happened. But he shook his head. "Carter, I'm sorry. Something like that"—he blew out his breath—"he could claim he was moving into position for a catch, or say he didn't know Carter was trying for a double, or that he just lost his balance and had to move his foot to stay up." He turned to Carter. "I know it's hard to accept, but these things happen. What's important now is that you put it behind you so you can focus on the challenges ahead. Okay?"

Carter nodded. But he didn't look happy as he headed to the mound.

Liam wanted to explain to the coach that Carter had issues with Phillip DiMaggio, which was why he was so upset. But there wasn't time. He had to talk to his cousin before the inning began.

He suited up in his catcher's gear as quickly as he could and started out to the mound. But halfway there, he stopped.

Thud. Thud. Thud.

Carter was hurling the ball into his glove over and over. He wasn't doing it out of nerves this time. The way he was glaring at the West team's dugout made it clear to Liam that he was channeling his anger.

Atta-boy, Liam thought, grinning as he jogged back to the plate. *I only hope you get to use that power against DiMaggio!*

CHAPTER
NINE

Carter didn't think he could be angrier than when his foot twisted on top of Phillip DiMaggio's. He was wrong. Since that moment, his rage had built until now it coursed through his veins like white lightning, pulsing hotter with every beat of his heart.

Get ready, Liam, he thought, *because these throws are going to sizzle.*

The first batter came to the plate. Carter rocketed in three fastballs, all strikes and all too hot for the batter to handle. The West player left the box with such a dumbfounded look on his face that Carter almost pitied him.

Almost.

The fans whooped their appreciation. Carter blocked out the cries and focused on the next batter.

This time, he followed up a blistering four-seam fastball—another strike—with a slow-moving changeup. The batter fanned at that one as well, and when he failed to connect with the third pitch, Carter had notched the second out for the team.

"Now batting," the announcer cried, "Phiiil-lip DiMaggio!"

All right, DiMaggio, Carter said to himself. *You got a homer last time, but this time, I'll tell you what you're going to get. A big fat nothing, that's what!*

He ran over his experience with DiMaggio. His last at-bat, he'd aimed two fastballs to the outside corner. Both had been called balls, but DiMaggio hadn't even tried for them. Was his eye that good, or was that a pitch he had trouble hitting?

Carter wanted to find out and was pleased when Liam flashed one finger and tapped the inside of his right thigh. This time, Carter's aim was true. The ball whizzed in low and caught the corner just inside the strike zone.

"Steee-rike!" the umpire bellowed, making a hammering motion with his right fist.

One down, two to go, Carter thought.

DiMaggio stepped out of the box and fiddled with his batting helmet, then his glove.

Liam plucked the ball out of his mitt and heaved it back, shooting Carter a wide grin. Carter responded by narrowing his eyes.

Save it for after we've won the game, his intense stare said. Liam's smile vanished, and Carter knew he'd understood.

Phillip got back into place and lifted the bat. Liam signaled for the same pitch, fastball low and outside. This time, Carter shook him off.

He's smart. He'll be looking for a repeat of the one that got by.

Liam flicked out three fingers, their signal for a changeup. Carter nodded. With the ball hidden in his glove, he switched his grip. Now his three middle fingers were draped across the seam on top. His pinky and thumb cradled the ball below, anchoring it firmly against the palm of his hand. Then he went into his windup exactly as if he were about to throw a fastball. But instead of hurtling toward the plate, the changeup floated at a fraction of the speed.

Whap! DiMaggio got a bite out of it, not a powerful blast, but enough to lift the ball over short. John Harper had replaced Miguel at shortstop. Not as tall as Miguel,

John made a desperate leap to try to catch it. He missed, but his glove poked the ball. That poke redirected its path away from Oliver, who had sprinted in from center field to capture it!

The fielding flub was costly. Now the West had a runner on first, dusting off his pants and smirking like the cat that had swallowed the canary.

Carter slapped his glove against his thigh. *DiMaggio is safe on first, but he sure isn't going to reach second.*

With two outs, he knew it was possible the West's coach would signal his runner to steal. That's where being a left-handed pitcher was an advantage. Unlike a righty, who had to look over his shoulder to check the runner, Carter faced first. He'd be able to keep an eye on DiMaggio.

Sure enough, as Carter brought the ball up, he saw movement. Quick as a wink, he rifled the ball to Jerry Tuckerman. Not fast enough, though. DiMaggio dove back to the bag, safe.

Twice more, Carter switched his pitch to a pickoff attempt. Twice more, DiMaggio beat the throw. Carter felt his frustration mount with each failed attempt.

"Time!"

Liam trundled up to the mound, a puzzled look on his face. "What gives, man?"

"What do you mean? I'm keeping DiMaggio honest!"

Liam's forehead creased into a deep frown. "I don't think he's really planning to steal, though."

Carter blinked rapidly. "Then what—" He paused as a thought shot through his brain. "You think he's trying to wear out my arm?"

"Either that or he's hoping to break your focus and knock you out of the zone," Liam suggested. "So how about you just pitch, and if he goes, I'll make the throw to second. Deal?"

Carter glanced over at DiMaggio, considering. "Okay," he said finally.

Liam nodded, pulled his mask over his face, and returned to the plate. Once he was in his crouch, he flashed the signal for a fastball right down the middle.

Carter glanced toward first once more and then went into his windup. He'd just snapped his wrist on the follow-through when he heard the crowd roar. He whirled around. DiMaggio was sprinting toward second.

"He's going, Liam! Get him!"

CHAPTER
TEN

Liam sprang to his feet and heaved the ball toward Ted Sandler at second.

Oh, no!

The throw sailed too far toward short. Ted lunged to try to make the catch, but missed. Luckily, Oliver was in the perfect backup position. He nabbed the ball and relayed it to Ted.

But Ted, forced to come off the base by Liam's bad throw, couldn't reach DiMaggio for the tag.

"Safe!" the umpire cried, fanning his arms out to either side.

Liam sank slowly back into his crouch. *I've made that throw hundreds of times,* he thought. *How could I have botched it?*

"Shake it off, Liam, shake it off!" he heard Coach Harrison yell. "One more out is all we need this inning!"

Liam gritted his teeth and nodded.

The batter had swung at Carter's first pitch. Now, with one strike on him, he swung at the second, another fastball down the middle. He missed that one as well. They needed just one more to disarm the scoring threat on second.

Carter looked in, wound up, and threw.

Pow! The batter creamed the ball, sending it flying high to right field! Craig Ruckel raced back, but to Liam's eye, it didn't look like he would get to it in time.

Craig wasn't the only Mid-Atlantic player on the move. Jerry ran to the cutoff position. Ted sprinted to cover first base. John darted over to second. And as the ball bounced onto the grass, Carter dashed past home, ready to back up Liam when the throw came.

Liam prayed that the throw would be on time and on target, for DiMaggio was churning up the base paths like a runaway locomotive.

In the outfield, Craig pounced on the ball.

DiMaggio rounded third.

Craig plucked the ball from his glove and threw to Jerry.

DiMaggio kept coming, his legs seeming to move even faster. Now he was halfway to home.

Liam stood in front of the plate, glove raised. Jerry caught the ball, spun, and threw.

Thud! The ball socked into Liam's mitt. He slapped his right hand over it, dropped to his knee, and swung around for the tag just as DiMaggio hit his slide. A cloud of dust plumed in front of Liam's face, but he didn't need to see to know where to aim his mitt.

But DiMaggio tricked him. Instead of a straight feet-first slide across the plate, he executed a perfect slide-past-and-reach-back maneuver. Liam's glove fanned the air as DiMaggio's hand dragged across the plate.

"Safe!" the umpire bellowed.

Liam wanted to die inside, but he knew his job wasn't over yet. He leaped to his feet and spotted the runner moving toward third. He hurled the ball to Leo Frick. Leo caught it. His glove flashed down and across.

Liam held his breath, waiting for the umpire's call. Was Leo's tag good?

"Out!"

The crowd roared, stomping and cheering madly. The inning was over, but it had been costly. Mid-Atlantic was now down by a run—and Liam knew he was to blame. He hoped to help his team pull away from the West in the bottom of the fifth, but DiMaggio retired the side in order, so he didn't get a chance at bat.

The West's leadoff batter in the sixth got on base with a clean single. But any idea the West players had of widening the gap in the score died when their next three hitters made outs.

Liam breathed a quick sigh of relief as he hurried to the dugout. Many of his teammates were already there, chattering in excitement.

"We need two to win," Coach Harrison reminded them needlessly. "One to go into extra innings. So take smart cuts, find the holes, and then run like the devil was at your heels when you connect!"

Mid-Atlantic was at the top of their order. John crammed on a batting helmet, chose his favorite bat, and strode to the plate. It was his first time up this game and he looked ready to make his mark. So when the pitch came in—*Whack!* He belted a low-flying grounder that skimmed the grass before taking a weird hop right in front of the shortstop's glove. Thanks to that hop, John reached first before the throw.

Now Jerry Tuckerman stepped into the batter's box. Up twice in the game, he hadn't reached base yet, and

Liam knew he wasn't likely to this time, either. Sure enough, the coach gave the signal for Jerry to bunt.

If Jerry was disappointed at not being allowed to swing away, he didn't show it. When the pitch came, he pivoted and knocked the ball straight down so it dribbled slowly toward the third-base line.

The West was expecting the play. The third baseman had already cheated onto the grass. Now he charged forward, scooped up the ball, and hurled it to first. Jerry was out, but John was safe at second.

The dugout erupted in cheers. "Way to be the sacrifice, Jerry!" Daniel Cho cried as Jerry returned to the bench.

Craig was Mid-Atlantic's next batter. Then it would be Liam's turn. He bumped fists with Carter three times and then grabbed a bat.

As Craig took his turn at bat, Liam watched DiMaggio pitch. Unless Craig hit into a double play, Liam was going to get a final chance against Phillip. He planned to make the most of it.

For the team, he thought, *and for me.*

Craig, an inconsistent hitter, surprised everyone by lofting the ball high and long. Not long enough, though. The center fielder backpedaled, raised his glove, and made the catch.

But while it hadn't been long enough to land beyond the outfielder's glove, it was far enough back to buy John running time. While the outfielder threw hard, John beat the ball to the bag, sliding safely into third.

Two outs. Tying run on third.

"Okay, Liam, you're up," Coach Harrison said, flashing him an encouraging smile. Liam smiled back and pushed a batting helmet onto his head. The roars of the spectators filled his ears as he approached the plate. He ignored them, stepped into the box, and lifted the bat over his shoulder.

Bring it, he challenged DiMaggio silently.

The first pitch was a fastball high and inside. Liam let it go by, certain it was a ball.

"Strike!"

Liam shot the umpire an incredulous look but didn't argue. The second pitch was to the same place and this time, Liam swung.

Tick! Foul ball up the first-base line.

"Steee-rike two!"

Liam stepped quickly out of the box. He tapped the bat against his cleats, knocking the caked-in dirt loose. Moisture gathered on his upper lip and he wiped it away. From the stands and hillside came a sound like rolling thunder.

Are they rooting for me, Liam wondered, *or against me?*

The umpire gave an impatient jerk of his head. "Let's go, son."

Liam stepped back into the batter's box and faced DiMaggio again. Their eyes met, Liam's dark brown clashing with Phillip's jet black, and suddenly the noise of the crowd fell away. Time seemed to slow. The only sounds Liam could hear were his steady breaths and the drub of his heart.

This pitch is mine, Liam thought.

DiMaggio wound up and threw. Liam uncoiled, swinging harder than he ever had, swinging for the fences, swinging for glory, for his team, for himself.

CHAPTER
ELEVEN

*T*hud. *Thud. Thud.*

Liam lay on the top bunk in Carter's bedroom, throwing a rubber ball at the ceiling over and over.

Carter watched him for a moment and then said tentatively, "Um, if that leaves a mark, my mom will kill you."

Liam sighed. Then he sat up and tossed the ball to Lucky Boy, who caught it in his mouth and wagged his tail. "At least someone's happy," he mumbled.

Carter bit his lip, not knowing what to say to that. In fact, he never seemed to know what to say to his cousin these days.

The Little League Baseball World Series had ended

more than three weeks ago. The West had won the title, beating the team from Japan six runs to four. Carter and his teammates had prime seats for the match.

Liam had begged the coach not to go. "Please don't make me," he'd pleaded. "I—I just can't show my face there, Coach."

And Coach Harrison, his eyes full of pity and understanding, had allowed Liam to stay away. "If anybody asks, I'll say you came down with something," he said kindly.

Carter figured that wasn't too far from the truth anyway—then, and now.

If only he'd hit it, he thought. *Or at least hadn't...*

He sighed, shaking his head to clear the memory. It stuck there all the same, playing like a rerun of a bad television sitcom. Liam swinging hard at the third pitch. Liam missing it by a mile. Liam corkscrewing around, carried by the momentum of his powerful swing, and falling flat on his face.

And the cameras catching every miserable moment, before, during, and after.

As awful as the strikeout was, it was the after that Carter found most difficult to think about. Liam had rolled over in the dirt and lay on his back, unmoving, while the West players jumped and screamed and celebrated their victory with Phillip DiMaggio, the game's hero.

Carter hurried out to his cousin's side. At that same moment, DiMaggio broke free and came to the plate, too. He crouched down next to Liam and offered him a hand up. The reporters had lapped up the gesture, praising DiMaggio for his thoughtfulness and good sportsmanship.

What a load of moldy baloney, Carter fumed now. DiMaggio hadn't come over to extend an olive branch; he'd come to deliver a parting shot.

"Hey, McGrath," he whispered, just loud enough to be heard by the cousins but no one else. He touched his finger to his chest and then his nose, imitating the nose-bop prank Liam had pulled on him two days before. Pointing at Liam, he smiled. "Made you whiff!"

Carter had been so stunned by the taunt that he hadn't been able to speak. It wasn't so much what DiMaggio had said, but that he'd said it at all. Little League had a motto of sportsmanship that was well-known to all players. First and foremost, they were expected to be respectful to others. With his words, Phillip had completely disregarded that code.

But Liam's and Carter's were the only ears it reached. Without proof, it would be their word against

Phillip's—just as it had been when Carter stumbled on the base path.

The sound of his mother's voice broke into Carter's thoughts. "Liam, hon, your mom wants you home for dinner in ten minutes."

"Okay," Liam called back. Then he asked Carter if he wanted to come over to eat. "We're having tacos, I think."

Carter loved tacos, but when they went downstairs and asked his mother for permission, she shook her head.

"Sorry, Carter, but not tonight," she replied. "School tomorrow, remember?"

Carter and Liam had started at the middle school two weeks ago. Carter was still adjusting to his early morning wake-up time, not to mention his teachers and homework load. The only plus so far was that he and Liam shared a few classes. Since they went to one or the other's house every day after school, they were able to do their homework together.

"I guess I'll get going then," Liam said. "See you tomorrow, Carter. 'Bye, Aunt Cynthia. 'Bye, Lucky Boy."

Carter's mother smiled. "Don't forget to call when you get home, so I know you're safe!"

The reminder was an old joke between the families.

The boys had been traveling the short stretch of road between their two houses by themselves ever since they could walk. When they were younger, their mothers had insisted that they check in upon their arrival. Now, they said it to be funny.

Liam gave a polite laugh and then banged out the door.

His mother turned to Carter then. "How's he doing these days?" she asked, her eyes full of concern.

Carter lifted a shoulder and let it drop.

"I wish Amanda would get him to talk to somebody about it," she said. "Especially now that—" She stopped in midsentence.

Carter looked at her curiously. "Especially now that what?" he asked.

"Hmm? Oh, nothing. So, how do hamburgers sound? With French fries?"

Carter had the distinct impression that she was trying to change the subject. But his stomach gave such a growl at the mention of food that he decided it was better for her to focus on dinner than on answering more questions.

Twenty minutes later, he and his parents were enjoying a fine meal of burgers, fries, and steamed zucchini with butter. Their local farmer's market had had a bumper crop of the squash that year, and Carter had eaten so much of it that he was sure his skin was going to turn green. But since his mother also used it to make zucchini bread with chocolate chips, he didn't complain.

After dinner, he helped clear the table and then sat down to finish one last piece of homework. When he opened his binder, however, he discovered he didn't have the right worksheet. Luckily, Liam had the same assignment—and a printer with a copy feature.

His mother was in the shower, so Carter told his father that he was running over to the McGraths for a minute. His father, eyes glued to a ball game on the television, waved him away with a grunt.

"Come on, Lucky Boy, we're going to go see Liam!"

His dog leaped up and padded to his side. The night air was cool and pleasant, with just a hint of apple in the air from a nearby orchard. Carter sniffed and wished he'd grabbed an apple from the bag hanging in the closet. They were fresh-picked by his own hand two days ago, and nothing tasted better than that first crunchy bite!

He was still thinking about apples when he reached Liam's house. But what he heard inside drove away that and all other thoughts.

"What do you mean, we're moving to California?"

CHAPTER
TWELVE

Liam was sure he must have misunderstood. So he asked the question again, this time even louder.

"What do you mean, we're moving to California?"

He looked from his mother to his father and then to his sister. It was when he saw Melanie's expression that he knew he'd heard right. She was practically bursting with excitement.

"Southern California, the San Fernando area to be exact!" she cried. "Just think! Warm, sunny days all year-round! Swimming pools, beaches, and best of all—movie stars, television stars, cable-network stars! Isn't it awesome?" She sighed deeply and contentedly.

"No! It isn't awesome!" Liam retorted. He turned to

his parents. "When did all this happen? *Why* is all this happening? How come she knows about it"—he stabbed a finger at Melanie—"and I don't?"

They explained the situation as best as they could. Last summer, when they were in California, his mother had reconnected with some old friends from college. Those friends now designed and sold eco-friendly toys.

"I made some comment, a joke really, about how toys were small potatoes, that the big money was in eco-friendly playground equipment," she said. "But they took it seriously and asked me what such equipment would look like and how kids could play on it. So that night I sketched out some ideas and sent it to them."

"And they liked what you drew?"

She nodded. "They offered me a job in June. At first I said no, but they kept asking."

His father broke in. "After the third time, I reminded your mom that my company has a branch in the same area of California. If she wanted to take the job, I could get a transfer."

They'd learned the transfer had been approved just before the World Series tournament. They had decided not to say anything to him until after the Series was over. And with what happened there...

"Well, we decided to wait a little longer," his father said. "Was that the right decision? Maybe not. Then again, what would you have done if you'd known sooner?"

"I would have talked you out of it, that's what!" Liam cried.

"And I would have talked them *into* it," Melanie cut in. "Moving to Southern California will finally give me a real chance to pursue my acting career!"

Liam glared daggers at his sister. "Great, so she gets what she wants? And I don't even get a say?" He threw his arms in the air. "What about our lives here? What about this house and school and Carter and Aunt Cynthia and Uncle Peter? What about my Little League team?"

His father reached into his desk, pulled out a folder marked *Little League: Southern California*, and handed it to Liam. "They play baseball out there all year-round, buddy. In fact, their spring season starts in February, so you'll be there in plenty of time for tryouts."

Liam sprang to his feet. "Whoa, whoa, whoa, what do you mean, I'll be there in plenty of time? When are we moving?" He nearly choked on the last word.

His mother put her arm around his shoulders. "Right after Christmas," she said.

Liam couldn't bear to hear any more. He wrenched free of his mother, ran into the hallway, and flung open the front door.

"Liam!" his mother cried.

"Let him go," his father said.

Liam ran outside and smacked into someone standing on his front steps.

"Oof!"

It took him a moment to make out that it was Carter. "Did—did you hear any of that?" His voice cracked.

Carter nodded. "Not all, but enough."

They stared at each other. Then Carter started walking. "Come on. Let's go to the hideout."

Liam followed in a daze. At the edge of his lawn, he turned back and looked at his house, silhouetted against the purple twilight sky.

"I can't believe it. I'm...moving."

Lucky Boy, trotting at his feet, gave a small whine.

It took the boys fifteen minutes to reach their destination. The hideout was a natural shelter formed by boulders left behind by an ancient glacier. They'd discovered it one summer day when they were seven years old. That very day they'd made a secret pact to never tell anyone else about it, not even their parents. Since then, they'd brought a few things to make it more comfortable—a couple of old beach towels and two flashlights, sometimes food. They stored everything in a dark green plastic box with a tight lid. When the box was tucked deep underneath the overhang, it was impossible to see unless you were looking for it.

When they got to the hideout, they pulled out the box. As they were spreading the towels and checking the flashlights to be sure they still worked, Liam's cell phone rang. He took it out of his pocket and hit the "ignore" button. Then he turned it off completely and returned it to his pocket.

Carter looked at him questioningly. He shrugged. "Just doesn't seem like the right place for a cell phone, you know?"

"That's not what I'm wondering about and you know it."

Liam lay back on his towel and stared up at the sky. A few stars had popped out in the east, but the west still showed a nimbus of lingering light. Finally, he started talking.

"My life stinks," he said. "I lost us the game in Williamsport and looked like an idiot, too. You know that the clip of my strikeout is on YouTube, right?"

Carter picked up a pebble and threw it. "Yeah, I know. I was hoping you didn't, though."

Liam gave a short laugh. "Dude, I've watched it at least a hundred times. Every single time, I hope it's going to end differently. But it doesn't. And now we're moving."

A lump lodged in his throat. He flung his arm across his face to hide the tears that had suddenly sprung into his eyes. "What am I gonna do?"

Carter threw another pebble and then said, "You could hide here. Or in my closet!"

Liam moved his arm and stared at his cousin. Then he sat up. "That's it! Why didn't I think of that before? I'll live with you guys!"

Carter gave him a dubious look, but Liam was undeterred.

"Come on, it's the perfect solution!" he said. "Shoot, I'm at your house all the time anyway, and you've got bunk beds, and my folks could give your folks money for my food and stuff! Man, it'll be great! Like a never-ending sleepover!"

Liam grinned. The loss at Williamsport had been a blow, and the news about moving to California had threatened to derail him completely. But now he had come up with a plan, and suddenly he felt in charge again.

"Hey look, there's the Big Dipper!" He pointed at the sky. "That's my favorite constellation."

"Because it's easy to find?" Carter asked, craning his neck to look at the stars, too.

"Yeah. It's always right where it's supposed to be." Liam pulled Lucky Boy to him. The small dog's tail thumped in the dirt. "Kind of like I'll be after we talk to our parents—and that's right here in Pennsylvania!"

CHAPTER
THIRTEEN

Carter stared at the stars so he wouldn't have to look at the happiness on Liam's face. It wasn't that he didn't want his cousin to be happy.

I just wish he wouldn't get his hopes up so high, he thought. *Just because he thinks living with us is a good idea doesn't mean our parents will go for it.*

In fact, judging from the looks on their parents' faces later that night, they had expected the two of them to propose such a plan.

"I'm sorry, boys. We're not leaving Liam behind," Mrs. McGrath said. Her voice was kind, but firm. "This isn't just a trip. We're moving. And while we'll definitely be coming back for visits, there's no way of knowing if we'll ever move back here."

Carter's mother took Liam's hand. "I know it's hard, honey. Believe me, I know." She glanced at her sister. "Except for college, I've lived near Amanda my whole life. Now she's going to be across the country. It's not easy. Not at all. But it's the right thing for your family to do right now."

And that was that.

The weeks that followed flew by. Carter watched helplessly as the place he'd treated like a second home transformed into just another house. Rooms were stripped of all family photographs and repainted neutral colors. Garish clay pots and other homemade treasures that Liam had created when he was little were wrapped in newspaper and packed in boxes. The dining room table, usually strewn with newspapers, magazines, and crumbs from food long since eaten, was now covered with a new tablecloth and set as if company were coming for a fancy meal.

Even Liam's room was down to the bare bones. Gone were the trophies, the sports posters and team banners, the books, games, and toys he and Carter had shared since they were little kids.

"My dad says we have to make it look impersonal,"

Liam explained dully. "That way, it's easier for other families to imagine living here."

But I don't want another family living here! Carter wanted to scream. But he didn't have to; Liam already knew how he felt.

Throughout autumn, the only bright spot in Carter's life was playing baseball. Fall Ball in Pennsylvania wasn't as competitive as the summer league—there were no big tournaments or national competitions—but that suited Carter just fine. He used the weeks on the field to hone his skills and, whenever he could, boost Liam's spirits.

Those spirits needed boosting, too, for Liam was off his game throughout the short season. He played well enough behind the plate, but he had far fewer hits than normal.

"He's having trouble concentrating because of the move," Carter told their teammates whenever Liam was out of earshot. "Wouldn't you?"

His teammates had agreed. Still, Carter suspected they thought the real reason for Liam's slump was what had happened in Williamsport. He didn't blame them. After all, that's what he thought, too.

Fall Ball had been over for a week when, one afternoon in early November, the FOR SALE sign in Liam's front yard changed to SOLD. Carter and Liam raced up the steps of the house to find Liam's mother sitting at the kitchen table, stirring a cup of coffee and staring out the window.

"Someone bought our home," she said quietly. Then, to Carter's horror, his always cheerful aunt started to cry.

"Um, I think I'll go home and, uh, get started on my homework," he said, backing out the door. "You want to come, Liam?"

Liam hesitated and then shook his head. "No. But let's meet up later at the, um, you know?"

Carter nodded his understanding. He left Liam standing behind his mother, patting her back awkwardly.

That night, Carter sneaked out of the house. He met Liam at the end of his driveway, and together, they made their way through the woods to the hideout. It was a lot colder and darker than the last time they'd been there. Carter shoved his hands into his pockets and hunched his shoulders. Liam kicked at the hard ground.

"This is probably the last time I'll be here for a while," Liam said when they reached the shelter. "I mean, it's going to be winter for real soon. That means

Thanksgiving, then Christmas, and then..." His voice trailed off.

"Yeah." Carter shuffled his feet. "Listen, just so you know, I probably won't be coming here for a while either. I mean, call me a dork—"

"I always have."

"Shut up and listen, will you, you doofus?" Carter said. He cleared his throat and started again. "This is our place. It wouldn't feel right being here without you. There, now you can make fun of me all you want."

But for once Liam didn't crack a joke. Instead, he just said, "Thanks, man."

The McGraths hosted Thanksgiving that year because, as Liam's mother pointed out, they already had a table set for a fancy dinner.

"We might as well get some use out of that darned tablecloth!" she added with a rueful laugh.

"Okay," her sister agreed, "but dessert at our place!"

After a delicious turkey dinner with all the fixings, the Joneses and McGraths joined other neighbors for a friendly game of touch football. Then the two families piled into the Joneses' living room. Mr. Jones lit a fire, his wife served pie with ice cream and hot chocolate with whipped cream, and soon everyone was lolling about on the furniture, sleepy but content.

A few days after Thanksgiving, Christmas light displays and decorations sprang up around the neighborhood. The Joneses trekked to a nearby tree farm and chose a perfectly shaped evergreen to set up in their living room. The McGraths helped decorate it, because this year they wouldn't have a tree of their own.

Carter wasn't sure how Liam could stand it. No tree, no stockings, no outside light display, because all their Christmas decorations were already in California.

On Christmas morning, Carter called to ask Liam if he'd gotten any good presents. Liam snorted and replied, "Good presents? I guess if you think gift cards to a bunch of California stores I never even heard of are good, then yeah, I made out like a bandit!"

"Well, then come on over as soon as you can because I got you a real present," Carter said.

Liam barged in five minutes later, still wearing his bathrobe, slippers, and pajamas.

"Brrr, you look chilly," Carter's mother said when she saw him. She stuck a bright red Santa hat on his head, complete with white pom-pom. "There, much better."

"Mom," Carter said, rolling his eyes. "Leave him alone! Come on, man."

Carter led the way to his bedroom. He went to his closet and pulled out a large rectangular package wrapped in Christmas paper and decorated with a frilly ribbon.

"Nice bow," Liam commented. "Did you get it out of the new hair-and-makeup accessory kit you got for Christmas?"

"My mom made me stick that on, doofus," Carter said. He thrust the package into Liam's hands. "Here. Open it."

Liam did. Inside was a framed photograph. Liam studied it for a moment and then looked at Carter. "Um, it's...what is it?"

"It's an aerial shot of the area," Carter explained. He began pointing to places on the photo. "See, there's our school. That's the police station. That's your house and that's my house." He swung his finger to a wooded area beyond their houses. "And even though you can't really see it, that's where the hideout is."

"Wow. Oh, man, wow, Carter. This is really awesome!" Liam said, his eyes darting all around the photo. He gave Carter an apologetic look. "I didn't get you anything. Oh, wait, yes I did!" He reached into the pocket of his robe, rooted around, and pulled something out. "Hold out your hands."

Carter did as he was told. Liam dropped a fuzzy ball of lint into his cupped hands. "There's more where that came from, if you play your cards right!"

Carter looked from the lint ball to his cousin and burst out laughing. "Merry Christmas, doofus."

"Merry Christmas, dork."

Two days later, the McGraths were gone.

CHAPTER
FOURTEEN

Your webcam is just picking up the top of your head," Liam said with a grin. "Move it down a bit." He watched his laptop screen as Carter's image shifted into better view, then added, "Nice haircut. Glad to see you're keeping up your dorky appearance."

"Speaking of appearances," Carter replied, "take a look at yourself, doofus. What's with the clothes?"

Three weeks had passed since Liam and his family had moved to the San Fernando Valley. He and Carter had talked and texted several times. Now they were testing out Skype, a video-chat service their parents had agreed to let them use.

Liam glanced down and groaned. He'd forgotten he was in his school uniform.

Back in Pennsylvania, he'd worn T-shirts and jeans to school every day. Here, he was enrolled in a private academy because, his parents said, they didn't want him to get lost in the big public school. The academy wasn't bad except that all the boys were required to wear a light blue button-down shirt, a school tie, and khaki pants every day. The girls had similar outfits, except instead of pants, they wore plaid skirts.

"I have to wear it for school," he mumbled, yanking off the tie and throwing it across the room.

"Yikes," Carter said, laughing. "So what's your fancy-schmancy school like, anyway?"

Liam shrugged. "It's all right, I guess. Some of the guys seem pretty cool. The cafeteria food is decent. The teachers are okay. How're things back home?"

Carter's smile vanished. "They moved in last weekend."

"Oh." Liam knew *they* were the people who'd bought his house. "And?"

"And it's totally freaky seeing them going in and out of your home," Carter said. "They have a boy our age. His name is Ashley."

Liam made a face. "*Ashley?* Blech. Who does that to a kid?"

"Mom heard that he goes by Ash."

"Still. Does he play baseball?"

Carter shrugged as if he didn't know or care and changed the subject. "What's going on with your baseball stuff, anyway?"

"I get evaluated the day after tomorrow," Liam said. "Then practices start in February and the regular season begins in March."

Carter looked confused for a moment. Then his expression cleared. "I keep forgetting the weather is different out there. We've got six inches of new snow here and it's still coming down."

"Lucky! I've got exactly none, unless you count what's up in the mountains."

"Yeah, but you get to play baseball outdoors in January," Carter countered. "If I want to get in any playing time now, I have to go to that indoor sports place. And it might not even be open. Last time my mom and I drove by it, there were construction trucks everywhere."

"They're probably there to tear it down. That place is a total dump!" Liam said.

"Remember that time we saw the bat hanging upside down from the rafters?"

Liam broke up at the memory. "We thought it was a

leftover Halloween decoration until it started flying around!"

"Those girls from the softball team were so freaked out they started batting at the bat with their bats!"

They were both laughing hard when Liam's aunt appeared on the screen behind Carter.

"Hi, Liam!" she said. "Sorry to interrupt the fun, but it's dinnertime here. And Carter hasn't finished his homework yet."

"Aww, Mom," Carter started to complain.

"We're having chicken parmesan and garlic bread."

"Oooo, gotta go, Liam!"

"Give everyone there my love and take some for yourself while you're at it," his aunt said.

"Sure will, Aunt Cynthia. 'Bye, Carter."

"See you, and good luck at tryouts!"

He held up a fist. Liam did the same. Together, they gently bumped their screens three times. Then Carter logged off.

Liam sat back and looked at the one decoration he'd put up in his new room: the photo Carter had given him for Christmas. He imagined the snow falling on his old house. Then he looked out his window at the bright sunshine, sighed, and moved to put his computer into hibernation.

His hand paused over the touchpad.

Don't watch it, he told himself.

But his fingertip seemed to have a mind of its own. Three taps later, a video began to play on the screen. He fast-forwarded to the final seconds of the clip.

"Bottom of the sixth inning of the United States Championship," a voiceover intoned. "Two outs, tying run on third, Liam McGrath at the plate with a count of oh-and-two. Here's the pitch and—*ooohhh!* McGrath has struck out! West wins the game and will move on to the title match of this year's Little League Baseball World Series!"

Liam rewound to the moment just before the announcer's gasp. He watched as he missed Phillip DiMaggio's pitch, spun around, and fell. In his head, he heard DiMaggio's whisper: "Made you whiff!"

He rewound again and watched a third time. Then a fourth and a fifth.

"Turn that off right now!"

Liam jumped at the sound of his father's voice. He'd been so focused on the disaster replaying in front of him that he hadn't heard his bedroom door open. Now his father strode into the room, reached over, and clicked the video closed.

"I told you not to watch that," he said. "One more time, and I'll take your laptop away!"

"Sorry," Liam mumbled, hanging his head.

"Don't be sorry." His father's tone was gentler, but still firm. "Just stop torturing yourself, okay? It's over, it's done, and it's time to move on. Right?"

"But what if I can't? You know how lousy I was during Fall Ball this year. I couldn't hit anything!" He slumped in his chair. "And now I've got tryouts in two days. What if I completely embarrass myself there by missing every pitch?"

He half-expected his father to tell him he was crazy, that he would do just fine on Saturday. But instead, Mr. McGrath nodded slowly and then asked, "What time do you get home from school tomorrow?"

"Around two thirty, I guess," Liam answered. "Why?"

"You'll see," was the only reply he got.

CHAPTER
FIFTEEN

Carter rolled over and opened one eye. The alarm clock on his nightstand read eight thirty-seven.

"Aaugh!" He shot out of bed and raced down the stairs to the kitchen. His parents were sitting at the table, sipping coffee.

"Mom! I'm late for school! Why didn't you get me up?"

"Because it's a snow day," she said, nodding with her chin at the window.

Carter spun around and stared. The landscape was indeed covered with a thick blanket of snow. "A snow day! Why didn't you wake me up and tell me?"

"Oh, yes, that would make sense," his mother said,

rolling her eyes. "I wake you up, just to tell you not to get up."

"Okay, okay," Carter grumbled good-naturedly. He looked out the window again. "A snow day! Awesome!"

"Mmmm," his father said. "Won't be that awesome in June when you're making up the missed day."

"Sheesh, Dad," Carter said, "how to suck the joy out of the room. I'm going to call the guys and see if they want to have a snowball fight!"

"Shovel the driveway first," Mr. Jones said as he got up to go to work.

"Aw, Dad, do I have to?" Then he caught the look on his father's face and said, "Right. Driveway first."

"Breakfast first," his mother amended. "Then clothes, *then* driveway. Snowball fight after lunch."

Carter grinned at her. "You got it, Mom."

He ate two bowls of his favorite cereal in five minutes flat and then called his friends before getting dressed. Most responded that they'd meet him at the middle school after lunch. Two yelled at him for waking them up before noon, but then said they were in for the snowball fight, too.

Ten minutes later, Carter was in the driveway with his shovel. The snow was wet and heavy, perfect for packing but difficult to push. He was glad when his mother came out to help. They had just finished clearing the last of it when she beckoned him to come over.

"Look," she said, "someone's coming out of Liam's house."

Carter glanced over. Sure enough, the garage door was opening and a boy about his age came out with a shovel. He looked at them, too, before beginning to push at the snow.

"Why don't you go offer to help him?"

Carter dug his shovel into the snow again and pretended not to have heard her. It didn't work.

"Please, Carter. It would be a nice thing to do, and a good way to meet him," she said quietly. "You could invite him to the snowball fight, too."

"I don't know, Mom."

She sighed. "Carter, I know it's not easy imagining someone else living in Liam's house. Believe me, I know. But the sooner we get used to it, the better. Look, his mother came out, too. Now we can both go over. Come on."

Carter had no choice but to follow her. Mrs. Jones greeted the woman brightly and apologized for not having stopped by sooner. "This is my son, Carter," she added.

"Hi," Carter mumbled.

"Hello, Carter, I'm Mrs. LaBrie," the woman said.

Her voice had a soft southern accent that reminded Carter of a movie he'd once seen about the Civil War. "That's my son, Ashley."

Ashley shot his mother a dark look and muttered, "*Ash*, Mom."

"*Ash* is in sixth grade," Mrs. LaBrie continued. "He was supposed to start today, but..." She waved at the snow.

"Carter is in the sixth grade, too," his mom said to Ash. "I'm sure if you have any questions about the middle school, Carter would be happy to answer them. Wouldn't you, Carter?"

"Yeah."

"And while we're on the subject of helping, can we give you a hand with the driveway?"

Mrs. LaBrie smiled. "I've got a better idea. Why don't you and I go inside for a get-acquainted cup of coffee and leave the boys to deal with the snow?"

"Inside...your house? Of course. Why not?"

Carter's mother gave him a meaningful look—*See, if I can do it, so can you,* that look said—and then followed Mrs. LaBrie into the house.

Carter and Ash regarded each other for a long moment. Ash was about Liam's height, Carter noticed, and had brown eyes, too. But the resemblance stopped there. Liam's hair was dark and covered his head like fuzz, it was cut so short. Ash's was white-blond and long enough to touch his collarbone, even with a hat on. It was hard to tell because of his snow jacket, but he looked leaner than Liam, too.

"Guess we should finish the shoveling," Carter said finally. "I'll take the end by the road."

As Carter began to work, he tried not to think about the last time he'd shoveled Liam's driveway. Then, he and his cousin had raced side-by-side to see who could finish his row first. Whoever lost was treated to a fistful of snow down the back. By the time they were done, they were both soaked through to the skin and laughing so hard they could barely stand up.

Now, he and Ash were at opposite ends and shoveling in complete silence. As he and Ash drew closer together to remove the final rows, Carter started working faster. He was dying to get the job done and go home. Finally, they were finished.

"Thanks," Ash said, taking off his ski hat and running his fingers through his hair. He looked at his house. "You want to come in?"

Carter tightened his grip on his shovel. Being inside Liam's house when it was stripped down to nothing had been bad enough. He didn't think he could take seeing it filled with some other family's belongings. "No, I don't think I should. I—I suddenly feel like I'm coming down with something." The lie burned in his throat, making his voice sound huskier than usual.

"Yeah, you don't sound so good," Ash said.

"I guess I'll just go home and spend the rest of the day in bed."

With that, Carter shouldered his shovel and left.

His mother returned home a few minutes later. "Well, Jeanne seems nice enough, but I must say it was odd being inside the house," she said, taking her jacket off and hanging it on a hook in the hallway. "What did you and Ash talk about?"

"Nothing," Carter said, then, seeing the look on his mother's face, quickly added, "We were too busy shoveling."

"Oh. Well, you'll have more time to get to know each other this afternoon."

"Ummm..."

She narrowed her eyes. "You did tell him about the snowball fight, didn't you?" When he didn't answer, she let out a huge sigh. "Oh, Carter. Put yourself in his shoes. Or Liam's. They're both in the same situation, after all, being the new kids in town. How would you feel if you found out no one was bothering to get to know Liam?

"Besides," she added with a mysterious gleam in her eye, "I have a feeling you and Ash have a lot in common."

"What makes you say that?"

"Go ask him to the snowball fight, and maybe you'll find out."

But Carter couldn't have invited Ash even if he'd wanted to, for when he opened the door, Ash and his mother were driving away.

Oh, well, he thought. *I tried!*

CHAPTER
SIXTEEN

*C*ome to the backyard.

Liam stared at the text on his phone in confusion. The message was from his father. But his father was at work. So why the message?

Only one way to find out, Liam thought. He headed down the stairs and opened the back door.

"Smile, Liam!"

Melanie appeared out of nowhere. She was aiming a video camera at him. The red light was on, indicating that she was recording.

Liam ducked out of camera range and spotted his father at the far end of the yard. "Dad!" he bellowed. "What's going on? What're you doing home? And what's she doing here and why does she have a camera? Or maybe I should ask why she's pointing the camera at me and not at herself?"

Their father jogged up. He handed Liam a wooden baseball bat.

"Tryouts are tomorrow, and you haven't hit at all since we got here. Well, now you will. I'll pitch. You'll hit."

"And Melanie?"

"Melanie has agreed to film you as you hit," his father said. "I'm hoping that when we watch the video, we'll be able to see what's going wrong with your swing. And then," he finished, "we'll fix it."

Liam loved playing ball with his father. A former player in high school, his dad still had a good arm and could swat a pitch farther into the outfield than any other father Liam knew, including Carter's. Even though he'd never coached a Little League team, he'd taught Liam a lot about the game.

But now, Liam wasn't sure he wanted to play. The last time he'd batted was in October during Fall Ball. His stats then hadn't been anything to write home about. And now, his sister was going to film his mistakes.

He knew his father was only trying to help. But he wished he could just go back inside and forget the whole thing.

Mr. McGrath had already put home plate in place. Now he counted out paces to where the pitching rubber would be in a Little League baseball diamond. He dumped out a bag of old baseballs, selected one, and then motioned for Liam to get ready.

Liam put on his batting helmet and stepped up to the plate. He tried to ignore Melanie, who stood a few feet away with the camera.

"Don't foul one into me," she warned. "This is brand-new equipment that I bought with my Christmas money."

Don't worry, Liam thought dismally. *I'll be lucky if I even get a hit.* But he just told his sister to take another step backward.

"We're just warming up here," his father called, "so these first ones will come in nice and easy." Then he wound up and threw. Liam swung and missed.

"That's okay, that's okay!" Mr. McGrath said. "Get ready for the next one."

Liam returned to his stance. The second ball flew toward him. This time, he hit it, but the point of impact sent the ball drilling right down into the dirt a few feet in front of him.

"Topped it that time," his father commented.

Liam bit his lip and readied himself again.

Mr. McGrath threw pitch after pitch. Liam hit some

of them, but none with much power. The rest he missed completely.

"Want to keep trying?" Mr. McGrath asked when he ran out of baseballs.

Liam swiped angrily at the sweat on his brow. "What's the point?" he said, his voice thick with frustration. "I won't get any better."

His father came to the plate. "Turn off the camera, Melanie, and upload the video onto my laptop, will you? Let me know when it's done."

"Sure, Dad."

Mr. McGrath waited for her to leave and then turned to Liam. "You're right. You won't get better. Not with that attitude, anyway."

Liam hung his head. "I know. I just don't know what I'm doing wrong!"

"Well, that's why we're trying this. I know it might not be fun for you to watch but—"

"Ready!" Melanie shouted from the house.

"Come on," Mr. McGrath said to Liam.

Liam didn't budge.

"You do know that professional athletes watch film of themselves all the time, right?"

Liam sighed. "Okay, okay." He fell in step with his

father. "Let's get this over with. Just tell Melanie to leave us alone!"

"Like I'd want to stick around and watch!" she said, flicking her long black hair over her shoulder and turning on her heel. When she was gone, Liam and his father sat at the kitchen table and watched the video.

"There's a lot that's *right* about what you're doing," Mr. McGrath commented after a few minutes. "Your stance is good, knees bent and body sideways to the pitch. Your grip looks right, firm but not clutching the handle. Your shoulders are level. From what I could tell when we were out back, your eyes were focused on me, so I'm pretty sure you were watching the ball all the way."

"I think I was," Liam said. "So if I'm doing all that right, why can't I hit like I used to?"

His father scratched his head as if puzzled. "I can't put my finger on it," he admitted. "But something about your swing is off."

It was while viewing his tenth attempt that Liam spotted it. "Hang on." He tapped the laptop's touchpad to pause the video.

Melanie had first started recording from a spot to the right of the plate. After the ninth pitch, she had shifted her position, switching to the opposite side on the left. They'd had a perfect view of his stance from her original position; now they could see what he did after his swing.

"Look!" Liam pointed to the screen in disbelief. "I didn't follow through."

"Let's see if it was just this one time."

Liam started the video again. They watched the eleventh, twelfth, and thirteen swings. Each time, Liam brought the bat around to the ball, but ended his motion there.

Liam's father snapped his fingers. "Yes! That's it!" he said, grinning. "You're hitting *at* the ball, not *through* it."

"That's why I'm not getting any power!" Liam finished excitedly.

Mr. McGrath nodded, but then turned thoughtful. "Hang on. Are you sure you used to follow through?"

Liam gave a short laugh. "Oh, yeah," he said. He opened the laptop's browser and typed in a website address. The video his father had insisted he never watch again popped up on the screen. Together, they relived the agonizing moment of his mighty World Series strikeout and his twisting fall to the ground.

"That's follow-through," Liam said when the clip ended. "If I'd stopped short, I would have stayed on my feet." Then he thought of something else. "I wonder if that's why I stopped following through in the first place. Maybe I've been afraid that I'll fall again."

"The mind is a pretty remarkable thing. Your sub-conscious could have taken over and prevented you from completing the swing," his father agreed. "But whatever the case, this is for sure: you need to find your follow-through again."

"And leave the corkscrew behind!" Liam added.

They grinned at each other. "You ready to give hitting another go?" Mr. McGrath asked.

Liam stood up. "Absolutely!"

CHAPTER
SEVENTEEN

Piff!

"Whoo hoo! Direct hit!" Jerry Tuckerman yelled.

Carter wiped the snow from his coat sleeve and grinned. "Oh, yeah? Take that!"

He hurled a snowball of his own at Jerry. Jerry ducked and the snowball flew over him.

"What's the matter, southpaw? Lost your aim or something?" Jerry taunted.

Charging toward his foe, Carter scooped up another handful and packed a snowball. "Stop moving for a second and I'll show you how good my aim is!"

As he'd hoped, Jerry backed away and right into an—

"Ambush!"

Daniel, Oliver, Miguel, and John popped up from behind a snowbank and rifled snowballs at Jerry. Jerry never saw them coming. *Whap! Whap! Whap! Whap!* All four missiles socked him square in the back. He pitched forward, landed on his knees, and died a dramatic mock-death.

"Yes!" Carter cried, pumping his fist and laughing. He and his friends had been battling for the past half hour on the field behind the middle school. Before the fight, the ground had been pristine, unsullied by a single footprint. Now it was churned up, packed down, and mounded up from the boys' snow war.

"Truce! Truce!" Leo called. He'd been hiding behind an equipment shack but now appeared with his cell phone in hand. "My mom says she'll have cookies and hot chocolate ready in ten minutes if we want to head to my house."

Leo lived just past the school. The seven boys agreed they were ready to take a break and so, moving in a pack, they made their way to the road.

Carter had just snatched Miguel's hat for a game of keep-away when a car drove past them. Mrs. LaBrie was behind the wheel. Ash was in the passenger seat. He and Carter locked eyes for a long second before Ash looked away, his lips tight. Then the car turned a corner and he was gone.

Carter felt about one inch tall thanks to the guilt that suddenly pressed down on him. *I did try,* he reminded himself fiercely. But he knew he was just lying to himself.

They arrived at Leo's house a moment later and in the commotion that followed, Carter pushed his guilt aside.

On Mrs. Frick's orders, they stripped off their wet snow gear in the garage before trooping into the kitchen. She poured out seven mugs of hot chocolate, tossed a bag of mini-marshmallows to Leo, and set a huge tray of sugar cookies in the center of the table.

"Have at it!" she said, backing away as if to save herself from a feeding frenzy.

The boys ate with gusto. Carter was midway through his third cookie when he spotted something interesting tacked to a bulletin board on a far wall.

"What's this?" he said, getting up and looking more closely at the colorful flyer. *You're Invited to the Grand Opening of the Diamond Champs!* the pamphlet announced.

Leo's mother answered. "Oh, that came in the mail today. Remember that old indoor baseball facility?

115

Apparently someone bought it and fixed it all up. The opening is tomorrow. You all probably got an invite, too. I'm sure the new owners sent it to anyone who's played Little League."

"Cool," Carter said. He read more and added, "Says the batting cages and pitching tunnels will be free to anyone who wants to try them. And no way! There's an indoor turf field, too, big enough to play real games on. You just have to bring your own glove." He turned and looked at his friends. "I think we should go check it out, don't you?"

His friends agreed enthusiastically. Then they polished off the rest of the cookies and made their way downstairs to play video games.

"The Diamond Champs," John said as he settled onto a couch. "I think I once read a book called that."

"You can read?" Oliver joked.

John threw a pillow at him, and with that, the war that had raged outside was renewed in the basement—until Mrs. Frick told them to knock it off.

Carter and his parents walked into the Diamond Champs the next afternoon. The place was bustling. Inside, shiny silver balloons in the shapes of balls, bats, and gloves danced everywhere. Music blared from loudspeakers. Employees dressed in baseball uniforms handed out paper cones of buttered popcorn, hot dogs, and sodas. The sights, sounds, and smells reminded Carter of a stadium during a game.

"I think I'm going to spend a lot of time here," he said with a grin. "A lot of money, too!"

"In that case," his mother said, "maybe we'd better say hello to the owner. There she is."

Carter looked where she was pointing—and gulped. "Mrs. LaBrie?" he said, staring at their new neighbor. "*She* bought the place?"

Mrs. Jones nodded. "I didn't tell you because I didn't want you to get to know Ash just because of this." She indicated the facility. "I know I can't insist you be his friend, Carter. But I think you'd agree that you do have something in common."

Carter shrugged noncommittally. Then he followed his parents to the counter. Mrs. LaBrie greeted them warmly. "Cynthia, Carter, nice to see you again. And you must be Peter?"

While the adults chatted, Carter looked around. *Ash must be here somewhere,* he thought. He hoped he'd see him before Ash saw him. That way, he could duck away if he wanted.

Just then, he heard someone call his name. Jerry,

Ted, and Remy hurried toward him. All three were sweaty and grinning.

"Carter, you have got to try out one of the batting cages!" Jerry said. "Brand-new, state-of-the-art pitching machines that actually *pitch balls*! Not like those old loser ones, where the balls just fell out of the opening onto the floor, remember? Come on!"

Carter told his parents where he was going and then followed the other boys. He couldn't see the cage because there were too many people in the way. But he knew they were near when he heard a familiar sound.

Thock!

The crowd cheered and applauded.

"That sounded like a dinger! Who's batting?" Carter craned his neck to see around the people in front of him. "Anyone we know?"

Then the crowd parted and he saw who was at bat. It was Ash. As Carter watched, the machine rocketed out another fireball of a pitch. Ash swung and creamed it.

"Whoa, did you see that?" Jerry cried. He turned to Carter with a look of excitement. "You know who that is?"

Carter was about to say that the boy's name was Ash, but that's not what Jerry meant.

"That," Jerry said, "is the guy we're going to get to replace Liam!"

CHAPTER
EIGHTEEN

Liam looked around at the ballplayers sitting with him in the stands. He stifled a yawn, but it wasn't easy. Baseball tryouts for kids with last names starting with A through M had started twenty minutes ago. But so far, all they'd done was listen to a man named Dr. Driscoll.

Dr. Driscoll started out by explaining that he had taken over as the director of their district's Little League Majors division because the previous head had moved up to the Juniors to coach his thirteen-year-old son. He went on to tell them that their league had enough players to field seven teams. He reminded them that at the end of the regular season, the best players from those teams would be selected for their league's All-Star team.

Finally, he put his clipboard aside. "Now let's see what you can do! Everyone has their number pinned to their backs?"

Liam murmured *yes* along with the rest of the boys.

"Good. Numbers one through twenty-five stay here with Mr. Madding"—he indicated a pudgy man with glasses and a goatee—"for batting evaluation. Twenty-six and higher, get your gloves and come with me to the outfield."

Liam, number twenty-seven, made his way down the stands. He stood to one side as the batters hurried past. One of them glanced at him—and then did a double take, staring at Liam until the wave of boys pushed him onward.

Liam blinked. The boy seemed to know who he was, but Liam was sure he'd never seen him before. *Maybe he goes to my school,* he thought.

Fielding evaluation was divided into four categories: snaring a ground ball, throwing to first, catching at first, and catching fly balls. Liam was put with a group of six other boys and instructed to find a spot in the outfield. There, a pitching machine was set up, its nose pointed skyward. Liam knew it would soon be shooting balls into the air for them to call and catch. But right now, Dr. Driscoll was having difficulty making the machine work.

"Hi, you're Liam, right?"

Liam turned to see a short boy with red hair and freckles smiling at him. He recognized the boy from his new school. "Yeah. And you're Sean, aren't you?"

"Yep, Sean Driscoll, and before you ask, yes, my dad is the one in charge, and no, I have no idea why he spent so much time boring a bunch of eleven- and twelve-year-old kids." Sean laughed. "But don't judge him on that. He knows baseball inside and out. Well, he knows the game inside and out," he amended. "He's never actually played before. But he's a good guy—"

"—if you do say so yourself!" finished another boy. He stuck out his hand. "Hi, I'm Rodney Driscoll," he added. "I see you've met my twin brother, Sean."

Liam's jaw dropped. He looked from Sean's red hair and pale complexion to Rodney's tight dark curls and chocolate-colored skin. "Twins?"

Rodney leaned in. "I'll let you in on a secret," he stage-whispered, "we're not identical!"

The Driscolls burst out laughing then.

"We're adopted," Sean explained. "And by some freaky coincidence, we happen to have the same birthday."

"We've been playing that twin gag for years," Rodney put in. "I'm still waiting for it to get old. So how do you like living here? What do you think of our school? Got a favorite movie?"

Liam was kept from answering by Dr. Driscoll's triumphant cry. The pitching machine was finally working.

The boys spread out on the field. Liam took a position between the Driscoll "twins" and waited.

The first ball shot up into the sky.

"I've got it!" a thickset boy to Liam's far left called. As Liam watched him hurry across the grass, he was reminded of a clip he once saw of Babe Ruth running the bases. Like Ruth, the boy looked awkward but got the job done, making a clean catch. His throw wasn't that strong, however. Instead of reaching Dr. Driscoll, it hit the ground and dribbled through the turf.

"Mendoza, you have *got* to find the power," Rodney called, shaking his head.

"That's why the god of baseball created the cutoff man!" Mendoza shouted back.

The pitching machine let out a loud beep. This time, the fly came Liam's way. He called for it, lifted his glove, and watched the ball all the way into the pocket. Unlike Mendoza's attempt, his throw socked into Dr. Driscoll's mitt.

Sean gave a low whistle. "Nice arm, man! You play outfield?"

"Actually," Liam said, "I play catcher. That's what I mostly played back in Pennsylvania, anyway."

Rodney gave a short laugh. "Huh, well, don't get your hopes too high. You'll be going up against some tough competition," he said. "Most of these guys have been in the league for years, and these coaches know them already so—"

"—I have to really show them something good today," Liam finished.

"Read my mind," Rodney said. Then he was off to make a catch.

Liam wasn't particularly troubled by what Rodney had said. After all, players were expected to shift around in different positions, and he'd spent a fair amount of time in the outfield. Still, the thought that he might not play catcher at all did make him step up his play during the remainder of the fielding evaluation. He made one or two mistakes, but nothing major.

Then it was his group's turn to show what they could do at the plate.

Follow through, Liam thought as he waited in line. *Don't forget the follow-through!*

Thanks to his father and a few more hours of practice in the backyard, Liam was feeling much more confident as he took some practice cuts. *Plus,* he thought as he grinned at Sean and Rodney, *I'm finally making a few friends in this town!*

"Go get'em, Liam!" Sean cried.

"Liam? That kid's name is Liam? Oh, man, I knew he looked familiar!"

Liam paused in midswing to see who had spoken. It was the boy who had stared at him earlier. He was staring at him again—and beginning to laugh.

"Don't you know who that is?" the boy said, his voice full of mirth. "That's Major Whiff! You know, the guy who struck out at the World Series last year? The guy who swung for the fences, but hit the dirt? That's *him*! *That's* Major Whiff!"

And just like that, Liam's world came crashing down.

CHAPTER
NINETEEN

The pitching machine gave a final whir and then shut down.

"Aww," the crowd said as one. But Ash made it clear he was done hitting when he took off his batting helmet. That's when Jerry rushed up to him.

"Tell me that you're going to play Little League," Jerry said, his voice pleading. "And that you're the right age to play in the Majors!"

Ash looked startled by Jerry's aggressive enthusiasm.

Jerry didn't seem to notice. "Obviously, you've played before," he said. "What position? And if you say catcher, I may have to kiss you!"

Now Ash took a step back. "I've played catcher before," he said cautiously. "Um, who are you?"

"Your future teammate, if I'm lucky," Jerry said. "Carter, come here!"

Carter had shrunk back behind a group of people. But now he was forced to join the conversation.

"Hi, Ash."

Ash nodded but didn't say anything.

"Carter, how perfect is this?" Jerry crowed. "He can hit like Liam and he plays catcher like Liam!"

"He plays catcher," Carter corrected. "But we don't know if he plays like Liam."

"We can find out." Jerry turned to Ash. "This place has pitching tunnels, right?"

"Yeah, three of them."

"Well, Carter is a pitcher, you're a catcher, there's a tunnel—so what are we waiting for?" Jerry said. "Let's get you geared up and test you two out!"

Ash leveled a look at Carter. "I'm not sure your pitcher is interested. Maybe he's too tired after throwing snowballs all afternoon yesterday. Or maybe he's feeling sick again?"

Carter's face flamed beet red. "Jerry, I don't think this is such a good idea," he muttered.

"Of course it's a good idea," Jerry objected. "I thought of it, didn't I? Now come on, we're wasting time."

Ash shrugged. "I'm in if he is. The tunnels are this way."

So five minutes later, Carter stood on the mound waiting for Ash to finish putting on his gear. To his dismay, they had run into more of his teammates. Now practically the whole All-Star team was outside the netting with Jerry. All were watching with great interest.

"Let's see it, Carter!" Jerry cried.

Ash got into his crouch and pounded his mitt. Carter stared down the pitching tunnel, pondering which pitch to throw first. He decided on a straight four-seam fastball, but without full power.

No need to throw all my good stuff right away, he thought.

When Ash nodded that he was ready, Carter wound up and threw. The ball socked into Ash's glove with a satisfying thump.

"Whoo-hoo!" the boys cried as Ash returned the ball.

That felt good, Carter thought.

Ash set himself again. Carter repeated his motion and threw another strike. Again, the boys applauded.

Carter hurled three more pitches, all strikes. Then

Ash got up and removed his mask. Carter figured he was going to say he was through. But he was wrong.

"That the best you got?" Ash said. "I thought a famous World Series pitcher like you might have a little more heat."

Carter blinked in surprise. *Famous World Series pitcher? What did Ash know about that?*

He didn't have time to think about it because his teammates made an "oooing" sound at the challenge.

"You going to take that, Jones, or are you going to put a little more heat into your fastball?" Ted cried.

"Heat! Heat! Heat! Heat!" the other boys started chanting.

Ash dropped his mask in place. Carter pressed his foot to the rubber, leaned in, and rotated the ball until the stitches were beneath his fingers. Ash lifted his glove, showing Carter the target. Carter wound up and hurled the ball.

Whap! The ball hit Ash's mitt and stuck there.

The boys burst out in applause. "Are you kidding me?" Jerry crowed. "That had to have been fifty miles per hour!"

Carter grinned at them and then glanced at Ash with a triumphant look. But if he expected praise from the catcher, he was sorely mistaken.

"Not bad," Ash said dismissively.

"*Not bad?*" Carter echoed, his temper rising. "Do you know what the average speed for a twelve-year-old pitcher is?"

"Fifty to sixty miles per hour," Ash shot back. "So if Jerry is right about your speed, then I guess that makes you *average.*"

If Carter had been angry before, now he was downright furious. "Give me the ball," he said tightly. "And get ready."

Ash shrugged, flipped the ball to him underhand, and settled into his squat as if he didn't care what Carter did next one way or the other. Carter returned to the rubber and started throwing the ball into his glove.

Thud. Thud. Thud. Thud.

Remember: channel your anger into the pitch. Liam's advice suddenly sounded in his mind.

"Heat. Heat. Heat. Heat."

The chants, quieter now, pulsed in time with Carter's heartbeat. He turned and faced Ash.

Ash raised his glove. Carter focused on the pocket.

You want heat? I'll give you heat.

He went into his windup. Then, with a tremendous lunge forward, he rocketed the ball toward Ash. The pitch sizzled on a line and smacked into Ash's glove with a pop.

Jerry and the other boys jumped in the air, high-fiving and whooping as if they had thrown the heat themselves. Carter looked at Ash. Ash stood up and slowly removed his mask.

"That's more like it," he said. "That's the kind of heat that's going to get us on the road to Williamsport. And once we're on that road, we're going to put the pedal to the metal until we reach our final destination: the World Series Championship!"

CHAPTER
TWENTY

*M*ajor Whiff.

Liam's feet felt cemented to the dirt. He wanted to disappear. Instead, with the eyes of twenty-four boys on him, he approached the plate for his first at-bat of the evaluation.

Dr. Driscoll stood on the mound beside a different pitching machine. Liam stepped into the box. Dr. Driscoll pushed a button and the first ball flew out of the chute. Liam swung—and missed.

"That's okay!" Dr. Driscoll called. "Here comes the next one!"

Major Whiff. Liam tried to focus on the ball. But he hit nothing but air again.

"Eye on the ball, now, eye on the ball!" the coach encouraged.

Liam fanned the next three.

Dr. Driscoll adjusted something on the machine. "See what you can do with this one!"

This time, when the pitch came, it wasn't as fast. Liam connected for a bouncing grounder.

"There you go!" Dr. Driscoll praised.

Liam knew the coach meant well, but he was mortified. He had been hitting against pitching machines set at the fast speeds for two years. Having it set back to slow—and in front of a bunch of kids he didn't know—was humiliating.

He hit the remaining balls, and even rocketed one far into the outfield. But that was of little comfort. He left the plate feeling like a complete loser. For the first time in his life, he considered quitting baseball.

But just as the thought entered his mind, the Driscoll brothers chased it out.

"Dude, don't let it bother you," Rodney said.

"And don't let Robert Hall bother you, either," Sean put in.

"Robert Hall. Is he the kid who called me..." Liam couldn't bring himself to repeat the nickname.

"Robert Hall is an idiot," Sean said with great confidence.

"He spends half his time making fun of people," Rodney added, "and the other half trying to figure out why no one likes him. Seriously, forget about him."

Liam wasn't completely reassured. "But what if I get put on the same team with him?"

"If you are, don't let him know he bugs you," Sean advised, "because then he'll treat you like a scab."

"Huh?"

Sean flicked a fingernail across his arm. "A scab. You know, he'll keep picking at you until he makes you bleed."

Rodney made a face. "That's disgusting."

"Just saying."

Their easy banter and dismissal of Robert Hall made Liam feel better—temporarily. But the next morning, the nickname came back to haunt him.

Major Whiff. It sounds like "made you whiff."

Robert had seen the video of him striking out, that much was obvious. But there was no way he could know what Phillip DiMaggio had said to him afterward.

Carter and I were the only ones who heard that. The only way Robert would know about it was if we told him. Unless...

133

Liam sat bolt upright. "Unless he heard it from DiMaggio himself!" he whispered. But that would mean Robert knew Phillip. How could that be?

Dude, we're from the San Fernando area.

Liam's mouth turned dry as he remembered what Phillip's teammate had said in Williamsport. He jumped out of bed, booted up his laptop, and typed the words *Little League World Series* into the search line. A long list of articles and websites popped up. The second entry promised highlights of the most recent baseball tournament. Liam clicked on it and began to read.

Ten minutes later, he sank back in his chair.

My life is ruined.

His family hadn't just moved across the country. It'd moved to the same town as Phillip DiMaggio!

There's only one thing to do, Liam thought. *Get back in bed, pull the covers over my head, and wait for baseball season to be over.*

Just then, there was a knock on his door.

"Liam, some boys are here to see you," his mother called.

"Who is it?"

"Us." His door opened and Rodney and Sean walked in.

"We want to know if you like movies. How about hiking? Gold?" Sean asked.

The questions were so unexpected that Liam blinked. "If I like—? Huh?"

"We're on our way to a couple of parks around here, and we want to know if you can come," Rodney said. "One of them is Vasquez Rocks. They filmed a bunch of movie scenes there and you can hike around and see the locations."

"The other is Placerita Canyon," Sean put in. "It's got this big ol' oak tree that's supposed to have led to the discovery of gold."

"I thought gold was discovered in some mill."

"Sutter's Mill in 1848," Rodney agreed. "But gold was really discovered six years earlier by Francisco Lopez. Lopez fell asleep under the oak. He dreamed a golden river flowed underneath him. He woke up, dug around a bit, and voilà! Gold!"

"Huh," Liam said. "And the tree is still alive?"

"Come and see for yourself," Rodney said.

Liam glanced at his bed. As comfortable as it looked, he knew it wasn't where he wanted to be after all.

And, he realized, *the Driscolls must know something about DiMaggio.*

"Okay," he said. "Just let me get dressed."

Rodney waved a hand in front of his nose. "Consider brushing your teeth, too. It's a long car ride!"

Dr. Driscoll was sitting in the living room with Liam's father. To Liam's delight, his father had asked to join them on their adventure.

"I grew up around here," Mr. McGrath told Dr. Driscoll, "but it's been years since I visited those parks. Plus, I'm a huge *Star Trek* fan and I seem to recall several scenes from the original series were filmed at Vasquez!"

Liam rolled his eyes. "My dad's a total geek."

"I heard that," his father said.

"You were supposed to!"

Laughing, they piled into the Driscolls' minivan and headed for the hills.

Six hours later, the Driscolls dropped the McGraths back at their house.

"Thanks again!" Liam called. "See you guys at school tomorrow!"

Liam bounded up the stairs to his room, tired, but happy. The parks had been amazing, so different from back home with their dry, rocky terrain. They'd done a short hike to a waterfall and seen the oak tree, too. Liam's father had shared a few funny stories of times he'd been there with his own father. The day had ended with pizza and ice cream.

If Liam had been able to bring up Phillip DiMaggio, his day would have been perfect. But with his father there, he didn't dare. He just wanted to know if the Driscolls knew DiMaggio and whether he was playing Little League that season, and if he was, why he wasn't at the tryouts—not get another lecture about letting go of the past.

I'll ask the guys about him at school tomorrow.

CHAPTER
TWENTY-ONE

Sunday afternoon, Carter was sneaking a brownie from the kitchen when the doorbell rang.

"Can you get that, Carter?" his mother called from upstairs. "I've got an armful of laundry."

Carter shoved the brownie into his mouth and hurried to the door. When he saw Ash on the other side, he almost choked.

"Hey."

Carter swallowed hard to clear the thick chocolate wad from his throat. "Hey."

They stared at each other for a long moment. "So, can I come in?" Ash finally said.

Carter flushed. "Oh, yeah, sure."

Ash stepped inside. Carter closed the door and led the way into the living room. Ash sat down and looked around. He pointed to a photograph on a nearby shelf.

"Is that the guy who used to live in my house?" he asked.

The photo was of Carter and Liam, arms around each other's shoulders. It had been taken last season, just after they'd won the Regional Championship game. They were both in uniform. Liam still had his catcher's gear on.

Ash nodded as if he already knew the answer. "When Mom told me we were moving to this town, the first thing I did was check out your Little League," he said. "I read about you guys all summer. I watched all the World Series games online and read the player profiles on the Little League website." He jerked his chin at the photo. "He was your cousin or something, right?"

"He still is," Carter said.

"Yeah, of course. That was dumb, huh?" Ash went to the shelf and picked up another photo, this one of the whole All-Star team. "Most of these guys will play again this year, right?"

Carter shrugged. "I guess."

"And they'll be All-Stars again, too. At least that's what your coach, Mr. Harrison, said. But you'll be missing a key player." Ash stabbed a finger at Liam's image. "He's gone. That's where I come in."

He sat back down, leaned forward, and stared intently at Carter. "I want to be your catcher this year. I think you and I would make a good team. We worked okay together yesterday anyway, and with practice we'll only get better. In fact, I bet with you on the mound and me behind the plate calling the shots, we'll take the title in Williamsport."

"Oo-o-kaay," Carter said slowly. To himself, he added, *What planet is this guy from?*

"Obviously, we can't control whether we get on the same team," Ash continued. "But just in case we do, we should start getting in a groove by practicing now."

"I guess," Carter said again.

Ash slapped his hands on his thighs. "Good. I'll reserve an hour in the pitching tunnels for tomorrow night. My mom will drive us." And then, without waiting for Carter to respond, he stood up and left.

Carter sat in his chair, blinking in confusion. "What just happened?" he asked the air.

"I was about to ask you that," his mother said, poking her head into the doorway. "Was that Ash? What did he want?"

"He wanted to talk about baseball," Carter replied.

His mother smiled. "Great! Glad you two are connecting." She swept away with another load of laundry.

Connecting? Carter thought. *Is that what we did? Because it felt more like being run over by a Mack truck!*

He picked up the photo of him and Liam. Loneliness suddenly hit him like a ton of bricks. He put the picture back on its shelf, hurried to the hallway, and put on his coat, mittens, and boots. "Mom, I'm taking Lucky Boy for a walk!" he called. He jangled his dog's leash. Lucky Boy came running and the two set off together.

Snow had started falling, a gentle white powder that drifted softly all around him. Carter scuffed through it past the house between his and Liam's—*and it'll always be Liam's, never Ash's,* he thought bitterly—then darted into the woods.

The light inside the forest was dim, but Carter knew his way.

He had stayed away from the shelter ever since Liam had moved. But now, he strode purposefully through the snow, picking up his pace the closer he got. Lucky Boy trotted along beside him, his nose to the ground. And then they were there.

The hideout was exactly as they had left it, with the dark green box wedged up in the back. He dragged it out and spread one of the towels on the ground beneath the overhang. Then he sat down and watched the snow fall. Lucky Boy sat down, too, but he watched Carter, his liquid brown eyes seemingly filled with concern. Carter took off his gloves and stroked his dog's silky ears.

"I'm all right, Lucky Boy. I'm—"

Crack!

The loud snap of a branch breaking sounded like a gunshot. Carter sat very still, listening. A second snap echoed up the trail.

Someone was coming. He quickly edged farther beneath the shelter and urged Lucky Boy to follow. He held his breath, certain that if he just kept still he wouldn't be detected.

But whoever was out there was getting closer.

All at once, Carter understood. *Our footprints! They lead right to the hideout!*

He and Liam had sworn never to reveal their secret place to anyone. If he didn't do something, it would be his fault that it was discovered.

Moving as quickly and quietly as possible, he scooped up Lucky Boy and slipped from the shelter, pulling the towel behind him as he did to obliterate his tracks. When he was far enough from the opening, he balled up the towel and threw it under the overhang. To his relief it landed far at the back, out of sight.

Then he put Lucky Boy back down, began walking briskly back down the trail—and almost had a heart attack, for there was Ash, coming straight toward him.

"What are you doing out here?"

Ash brushed the snow from his coat and hair. "I saw you take off into the woods and wanted to see where you were going." He peered beyond Carter. "What's up there, anyway?"

"Just more woods." Carter pushed past Ash and headed back down the path. "Listen, want to come back to my house for some hot chocolate?"

After what seemed like an eternity, Ash turned back and said, "Nah. I've got homework to finish. See you at school."

CHAPTER
TWENTY-TWO

Yeah, we know Phillip."

It was Monday. Liam had cornered the Driscoll brothers at lunch and asked them about Phillip DiMaggio.

"He's playing in the Majors," Sean continued. "He missed our evaluation because he had to go to a funeral up north that day. But he made the second one, so he'll be on a team."

Liam put his sandwich down, his appetite gone.

Sean and Rodney exchanged glances. "There's something else you should know," Rodney said. "We recognized you when you started school here. We've seen the video clip of your strikeout. Heck, everyone who followed the Little League World Series last year has seen it."

Now Liam hadn't just lost his appetite. He thought he might throw up. "Why didn't you tell me all this yesterday? Or at the tryouts?" he asked miserably.

Rodney put his milk down. "Because we figured you'd want to forget all about that strikeout and start fresh."

Sean nodded. "We're big believers in fresh starts. We told you we're adopted, right? Well, we weren't babies. We'd been bouncing around the foster-care system for six years. Probably still would be if it weren't for Dad."

"He's a dentist," Rodney said. "He did a talk about dental hygiene at our elementary school, made us all demonstrate how we brush. I guess we failed, because afterward he demanded to talk to our parents. He found out we didn't have any."

"Long story short," Sean said, "we went to live with him. One year later, he adopted us."

"That was our fresh start," Rodney said. "We thought you'd have yours when Phillip didn't show up at our tryouts, and when no one else recognized you."

"But Robert figured out who I was," Liam said. "And DiMaggio is playing. So good-bye, fresh start."

The Driscolls looked grave. "You're not going to quit, are you?" Sean finally asked.

Liam frowned and shook his head. "And look like I'm scared to face him? No way. But man, I hate the thought of seeing him again. And what am I going to do if I end up on his team?"

"Well, you won't have to wonder about that for too much longer," Rodney said. "The draft is tonight. We should find out our teams by tomorrow."

When Liam got home that afternoon, he discovered his mother in the family room surrounded by large-scale drawings of playgrounds. She held one up for his inspection. "What do you think—curly slide or long tube from this second level?"

"How about one of each?" Liam suggested. "That way, kids can race each other down them."

"Love it!" she crowed, grabbing a pencil and sketching furiously. "How was school?"

"Well, I learned something today," he replied.

"Since that's the point of school, that's good."

"Yeah, except what I learned isn't good." He sank down in his favorite recliner and told her everything the Driscolls had told him.

She covered her mouth in horror. "Oh, honey, if we'd known he lived here—"

"It's okay, Mom," Liam broke in. "I can handle it. I just figured I should tell you."

"I'm glad you did," she said. "And Liam? If there's anything I can do, tell me that, too."

"I will." He shouldered his backpack and trudged up to his room. He took out his homework but didn't start on it. Instead, he fired up his computer, logged onto Skype, and called Carter.

Carter's image appeared a moment later. "Doofus! Working hard or hardly working?"

"Supposed to be homeworking, but I had to tell you something first. Are you sitting down?"

"Ooo, this sounds serious!"

"Just listen, okay? I find out who's on my team tomorrow. One of the players might be someone you know."

Carter laughed. "How would I—?"

"I could be on a team with Phillip DiMaggio."

The color drained from Carter's face. "No. Come on, Liam, you're joking, right?"

"You see me laughing?" Then Liam told him what he'd found out that day. Carter sagged back in his chair. "It's—that's—oh, man, Liam."

"Yeah." Liam sighed. "On the bright side, I'm getting

to be friends with Rodney and Sean, so at least there's someone around here who will hang out with me. Speaking of which—what's the latest news on Ashley?"

"Oh, you know, he's just...you know, a new kid," Carter replied. "Mom's making me be nice to him."

Just then, Liam heard Lucky Boy start barking. "I know that bark. Someone's at your door," he said with a smile.

"Yeah, and Mom's not home so I better go answer it," Carter said. "Skype, text, or call when you get your team assignment, okay?"

"I will."

"And don't forget, Liam." Carter touched his finger to his chest and then bopped himself in the nose. "You surprised DiMaggio once before. You can do it again, only this time, on the ball field."

Liam laughed, bumped screen fists three times with his cousin, and signed off. Then he sat back and thought about what Carter had said. After a few minutes, he got up and hurried downstairs.

"Hey, Mom, I thought of something you can do."

"Name it."

"Pitch to me. As many pitches as your arm can take. And when it wears out, take me to the batting cages and leave me there until I run out of money, the machines run out of balls, or the place closes for the night."

She smiled broadly. "Sounds to me like you have a plan."

"You bet I do. Major Whiff is going to surprise Phillip DiMaggio and everyone else by turning into Major Hit!"

CHAPTER
TWENTY-THREE

Ash pulled off his catcher's mask and gave Carter a long look. "That's the fifth one outside the strike zone. Are you going to pitch for real or not?"

Carter and Ash had been in the Diamond Champs pitching tunnel for twenty minutes. But Carter couldn't focus. Part of his brain was worrying about Liam and Phillip. The other part was worrying what Liam would think if he saw him pitching to Ash.

"It was a long day at school, so maybe—"

Ash held up a hand. "I get it. You want to quit, we'll quit."

The word *quit* hit Carter in the gut like a sucker punch. "I'm not a quitter."

"Good. Then get back to the rubber and throw some heat. I'll even sweeten the deal—three strikes in a row earns you the candy bar of your choice from the Diamond Champs concession stand."

"You're on."

Ash got into his crouch.

Carter reared back and threw as hard as he could.

Whap!

"Yeowch!" Ash took his hand out of his mitt and shook it, and then tossed the ball back to Carter. Twice more, Carter rifled in pitches that socked squarely into Ash's waiting glove.

"Yes!" Ash cried. "That last bullet was right on the money!"

"Speaking of money," Carter said, "you better have enough for that candy bar!"

Ash laughed. "As luck would have it, I'm in good with the owner!"

He threw the ball back to Carter. "Would you like to do it again? Hit six in a row and I'll throw in a soda with that candy bar. Of course, if you don't make it..."

"Yeah? What then?" Carter asked.

Ash raised an eyebrow. "You tell me what's in the woods behind our houses."

"What?" Carter said, flustered. "I already told you, there's nothing up there. I was just taking my dog for a walk."

"Then you don't have anything to lose, do you?"

Carter bit his lip. He felt trapped—and the only way to get free was to throw six solid strikes. "Get ready, then," he said finally, "because here comes the first one."

This time, instead of a straightforward fastball, he switched to a knuckleball. Digging the tips of his pointer, middle, and ring fingers into the ball just below the seam and securing the ball in place with his thumb, he focused on the target, reared back, and threw.

When thrown correctly, the knuckleball's flight is unpredictable, making it hard to hit. Unfortunately, it can also be hard to catch, especially if the pitcher puts any spin on it—which is just what Carter accidentally did. Ash had to lunge to one side to make the catch. Carter was angry with himself, but Ash just grinned and tossed him the ball.

"So, about the mystery in the forest—?" he asked.

Carter tried to think of something—*anything but telling Ash about the hideout!* But his mind was a blank.

After a long moment, Ash gave a snort. "Oh, forget about it! Come on, we still have some time before we have to get out of the tunnel. Why don't you try a two-seamer instead of the knuckleball, see if you can hit the target this time?"

Relieved yet feeling a pang of guilt for backing out, Carter nodded. He'd been throwing fastballs from the four-seam grip. But at Ash's suggestion, he changed now to a two-seam grip, rotating the ball so his index and middle fingers lined up parallel with the stitches instead of crossing perpendicular. This pitch, sometimes called a sinker, wasn't quite as fast, but Carter liked it because the ball didn't follow a straight line on the way to the catcher's mitt.

After ten sinkers, Carter switched his grip again, placing his middle three fingers on top of the ball and cupping it with his thumb and pinky below for a changeup. From a batter's point of view, the windup and delivery looked just like a classic fastball. But the grip made the ball come in at a much slower speed. Carter had learned the pitch at baseball camp and fooled many a batter with it since.

Now, however, he would have walked many because his accuracy was fading. After a third straight misfire, he decided it really was time to quit. He was about to say as much to Ash when the catcher stood up and jogged down the tunnel.

"How about making your final pitches all curve-balls?" he said, tossing the ball to Carter.

Carter stared. "Curveballs? You're kidding!"

Ash looked puzzled. "Why would I be kidding? Unless—don't you know how to throw one?"

Carter *did* know how to throw a curveball—in theory at least. But he'd never thrown one because Liam had warned him not to.

"There's something around your elbow that hasn't finished growing yet," he had once informed Carter. "Because of the way your forearm twists when you throw a curve, that thing can get all out of whack. Anyway, the article I read said you should wait until you're older and your body isn't growing and changing so much before you do the curve."

Carter answered Ash now, "I know how to throw them. I'm just not supposed to."

"Really?" Ash said with surprise. "Says who?"

"Says...says..." Carter paused, suddenly at a loss. Liam had said he shouldn't, but no coach had ever told him he *couldn't*.

"The pitch could be your secret weapon," Ash pressed. "Think about it: a good curve coming from a southpaw like you?" He held up his hands in mock surrender. "Batter beware!"

"I don't know," Carter said, still hesitating.

"Tell you what," Ash said. "Try one—just one—and I'll never ask you to tell me what's in the woods again."

That did it. "Give me the ball," Carter said.

With the ball nestled in his glove, Carter tried to visualize the pitch and the odd twisting motion his arm had to make for the ball to spin forward rather than backward. If thrown correctly, that spinning motion plus the speed of the ball would make the pitch drop before it reached the plate.

If done correctly, Carter thought. *That was the key!*

He took a deep breath, gripped the ball, wound up, and threw.

Thud!

It wasn't fast and it wasn't powerful. But the curveball dipped and hit Ash's glove as if drawn there by a magnet.

Carter's jaw dropped. "I—I did it!" he said wonderingly.

Ash leaped up with a huge grin on his face. "I knew you could! And I'll bet you could do it again, too!"

Carter flexed his fingers. "I guess it couldn't hurt to try," he said. *But only a few more times,* he promised himself silently, thinking again of Liam's warning. *And only to prove that the first one wasn't just beginner's luck!*

CHAPTER
TWENTY-FOUR

*Y*our *Little League Team Assignment: Pythons.*

Liam stared at the subject line of the e-mail. Then he took a deep breath and clicked on the message to open it. He scanned the contents quickly, passing over the information about practices, fundraising, and uniform requirements to get to the team roster.

He smiled broadly when he saw *R. Driscoll* and *S. Driscoll.* It made sense they were together, because their father was the Pythons coach. Someone named *J. Mendoza* was on the roster, too, and Liam wondered if it was the same Mendoza who'd reminded him of Babe Ruth at the tryouts. He didn't recognize any other name on the list—except for *R. Hall.*

Oh, great, he groaned inwardly. But his dismay at being on a team with the obnoxious Robert Hall was nothing compared with his relief at not seeing *P. DiMaggio* on the list.

I'll still have to face him on the field, he thought, *but at least I won't see him every practice and every game!*

The Pythons had their first practice three days later. Liam felt confident when his mother dropped him off at the field. Thanks to her help and extra time in the batting cages, his hitting had started to improve.

But his confidence faltered as he crossed the grass.

Several of his new teammates were gathered at the bleachers, laughing uproariously. One of them noticed Liam. He nudged another, who glanced over and then quickly whispered something to the others. Their laughter died as one by one, they turned to look at him. Their silent stares hit Liam like a bucket of cold water.

Then they parted and Liam came face-to-face with Robert.

"Well, if it isn't Major Whiff!" the burly boy drawled. "Come to show us your famous swing?" He took an exaggerated cut with an imaginary bat and then fell to the ground.

Don't let him know he's bugging you! Sean's advice echoed in Liam's mind.

Surprise him, he told himself.

"Actually, Robert, it was more like this." Now Liam pretended to miss a pitch, ending with a comical, slow-motion corkscrewing twist that made the other boys laugh out loud.

Liam smiled and stood up. "Yeah, not my finest moment," he admitted ruefully as he brushed off his pants. "But see, that's the thing. It was just *one moment.* And it was months ago! So how about we leave it in the past where it belongs? Or at least, judge me by how I play now instead. Okay?"

A few of the boys shuffled their feet. One or two shrugged. Others looked at Robert, who just rolled his eyes.

Not exactly the enthusiastic reaction I was looking for, Liam thought, *but it's better than having them laughing about me behind my back!*

"Little help here?"

Rodney, Sean, and Dr. Driscoll had arrived and were lugging mesh bags of equipment across the field. Liam and the rest of the Pythons hurried to lend a hand. Once everything was in the dugout, Dr. Driscoll introduced the Pythons assistant coach, Mr. Dumas, a tall balding man with a paunch and a thin mustache. Then he put his clipboard aside.

"We'll hit the field in a minute," he said. "But first, I'm going to teach you something very important." He looked around at them and smiled. "I'm going to teach you how to breathe."

"Seriously?" Robert exclaimed. "I've been doing that my whole life!"

A few of the players snickered.

"This is a different kind of breathing," Dr. Driscoll said. "Close your eyes. Now breathe in slowly through your nose. Hold it. Now let it out through your mouth."

He told them to repeat it while he explained the purpose of the exercise. "There will be times during games when the pressure will be tremendous. This breathing technique will help calm you. If you're calm, you can focus better. If you're focused, you're ready for whatever comes your way. Another way to stay focused? Between pitches, look at the webbing of your glove. It will keep your eyes from wandering."

Although he felt a little foolish, Liam did the breathing exercises because he liked Dr. Driscoll. Still, he was glad when they were over and the real practice began.

First up was a throwing drill. "Rodney, Sean, help me demonstrate the relay," Coach Driscoll requested.

The three formed a line with twenty-five-foot spaces between them. Rodney placed a ball by his feet. When his father yelled *go*, Rodney picked up the ball and hurled it to Sean in the middle. Sean spun and sent it to his father—who missed the catch.

"Whoops, my bad!" Dr. Driscoll retrieved the ball and threw it back to Sean. Or he tried to, anyway. Instead of hitting his son's glove, the ball flew far over his head.

"Been a while since I've thrown a ball, I guess," Coach Driscoll said.

"Yeah, like forever," Liam heard Robert mutter.

Liam shot him a look. Robert made a face in return and then, still looking at Liam, whispered something to the boy next to him. The boy flicked his eyes at Liam and hid a grin.

"You get the idea," Dr. Driscoll said. "Groups of three. Hustle, now!"

Sean motioned for Liam to join him and Rodney.

But instead, Liam moved between Robert and his friend. Before they could react, he swung his arms around their shoulders and squeezed.

"Thanks anyway," he called to the Driscoll boys, "but I'm dying to show these two what I can do."

CHAPTER
TWENTY-FIVE

Coach Harrison clapped his hands for attention. "Grab some turf and listen up!"

At the coach's command, Carter and his fellow ballplayers found spots to sit on the Diamond Champs indoor field.

"Welcome to the Little League tryouts," Coach Harrison said. "If you're here, that means two things. One, you're ready to play some ball. And two, your last name begins with a letter from A to M. If you're N through Z, you're a day early." He waited while the boys laughed and then continued. "As you know, our All-Star team had a great run last year, and I'm delighted to welcome many of those players back. But let me make one thing perfectly clear: All-Star team selection is months away. First comes the regular season. You want a chance to play on the All-Star team, you earn it by bringing your best to every practice and every game of that regular season!"

Murmurs of agreement rippled through the players.

"I'm not just talking about your skills, although obviously how you play is important. The other coaches and I will be watching you all season long. We're looking for the right attitude, sportsmanship, teamwork, and one hundred ten percent effort. Those are the elements that transform a good team into a great team! And that's what we want to see from you today!"

"Yeah!" several of the boys called out.

"We'll be ranking your ability on a scale of one to five in fielding, batting, and base running. Pitchers, you'll have a chance to show us what you can do, too. Now get out there and amaze us!"

The boys whooped and leaped to their feet. Carter was told to head to the batting cages along with fifteen others. Ash was among that fifteen.

"So, what do you think our chances are of getting on the same team?" Carter asked him while they waited for their turns at the plate.

Ash cocked his head to the side. "Oh, I'd say better

than average." He whirled a finger around at the batting cages and whispered, "Why else do you think I told Mom to let Little League use this place?" He gave a sly wink.

Carter stared at him. "You *bribed* them so we'd be put together?"

Ash burst out laughing. "Dude, tell me you know I'm joking!"

Before Carter could reply, Ash grabbed a bat and strode to the plate for his turn.

Was he joking? Of course he was joking. Wasn't he? Carter hoped so. But some little piece of him wondered. Then he thought of something. Even if Ash had tried to use the Diamond Champs as a bribe, there was no way Coach Harrison would have gone along with it.

Reassured, he selected a bat of his own. When it was his turn, he focused on the pitches shooting toward him. Some he missed, but the others he knocked into the nets at the far end of the tunnel.

After batting, Carter and his group moved to the turf for fielding. Carter took a turn at third base, his favorite position when not on the mound. He scooped up grounders, nabbed fly balls, and threw with as much accuracy and power as he could muster to players covering the other bases.

Base running followed fielding. Carter raced from bag to bag as fast as he could, cornering tightly and making sure he stayed within the base paths. After running, many boys were told they could leave. But Carter wasn't done yet.

"Pitchers, head to the tunnels and warm up!" Coach Harrison called. "We'll come check you out in a few minutes."

Carter felt a buzz of excitement in his gut. He started toward the tunnels. But then he stopped and knelt down as if to tie a loose shoelace.

I'll let the other pitchers go first so I can see how good they are, he thought. *Then I can decide if I need to impress Mr. Harrison with the curveball or not!*

Twenty minutes later, Carter had watched several young pitchers hurl fastballs and changeups. Most of them looked good. A few looked better than good. It was those few who decided it for Carter.

Prepare to be amazed, Coach! he thought as he strode into the tunnel. Ash partnered with him as catcher.

Carter didn't start with the curveball. Instead, like the other pitchers, he rifled in some fastballs, some changeups, and even a few knuckleballs. All found their mark, and Carter was pleased to see Coach Harrison nodding.

"Just as strong as last season, Carter," the coach said with satisfaction. "Maybe even stronger. One more, now, and we'll let the next boy have a go."

Carter nodded. Turning back, he caught Ash's eye.

Ash settled into his crouch and with a quick movement, flashed a sign.

Carter hid a grin. Carter wound up and delivered, twisting his forearm to give the ball the right spin. The ball hit Ash's glove cleanly.

I did it! Carter thought. *I—*

"Jones!" Coach Harrison's sudden bark interrupted Carter's thoughts. His tone was so different from just a moment ago that Carter's blood froze. "I'd like a word with you!"

Carter hurried out of the tunnel to follow the coach. The remaining boys whispered as he passed. "That doesn't sound good," he heard one of them say.

It wasn't good.

"Who taught you to throw a curveball?" Mr. Harrison demanded.

"I—nobody," Carter stammered. "I mean, I sort of taught myself." Up until that moment, he'd been proud of his accomplishment. Coach Harrison's disapproval sapped him of that pride.

The coach took his cap off and ran his fingers

through his hair. "Okay, Carter, listen to me. First of all, learning and practicing a new pitch—*any* new pitch—without guidance from a coach is not a good idea. More importantly, throwing curveballs can be downright dangerous to your arm."

Liam's long-ago warning about the curveball suddenly flashed through Carter's head. "Because I'm not old enough?"

Coach Harrison gave a rueful laugh. "If I had my way, I wouldn't allow anyone of any age to throw it. I don't care how effective a pitch it is. And don't get me wrong, it is effective or else no one would throw it. But it can also contribute to serious arm injury. At this stage of the game, you should be working on getting the ball over the plate consistently and changing speeds, hitting different points in the strike zone, and understanding what kind of pitches to use in different game situations. Leave the curveball for later in your career. Much, much later."

Carter swallowed hard. "Did I break a rule by throwing it?"

Coach Harrison narrowed his eyes at the question. "No, Carter, there isn't a written Little League rule prohibiting young players from throwing such a pitch. But let me assure you, if you're on my team this season, you will *not* be using it." He laid a hand on Carter's shoulder. "But no matter who your coach is, I hope you'll remember this: just because you *can* throw that pitch, doesn't mean you *should*."

CHAPTER
TWENTY-SIX

When Liam grabbed Robert and his friend—Scott Hoffmann was his name, Liam found out later—he'd just wanted to do something to zip Robert's lip. But midway through the relay drill, he realized he got something even better. He got an up close look at what Robert could do.

He wasn't impressed. Robert's throws had power, but his aim wasn't true. When he ran the bases during another drill, he looked so clumsy and slow Liam was reminded of a troll he'd once seen in a movie. He did okay at bat, knocking in some solid grounders and a few high flies, but nothing extraordinary.

In fact, Liam had trouble imagining Robert

contributing much to the team except a heavy dose of sarcasm. That, he had plenty of.

Scott, on the other hand, moved with fluid grace. He raced around the bases like a fleet-footed deer. While not particularly strong at the plate, he had a good swing, and Liam figured he was just out of practice. His throws were on target and powerful, and Liam wasn't surprised to learn that he was a pitcher.

What did come as a shock, however, was that Scott wanted Robert to be his catcher.

"Why him?" Liam wondered aloud at school on Monday.

"I think Scott is hoping Robert will turn out like his brother, Donnie," Rodney replied.

"Who's Donnie?"

Rodney looked surprised. "Donnie Hall? I thought you knew—Donnie Hall was Phillip's catcher at the World Series last year. He, um, he caught the pitch you missed."

"Oh, great," Liam groaned. "When do I get to face him?"

Sean laughed. "Don't worry, he's up in Juniors now, along with the rest of the World Series All-Stars. Phillip's the only one who was eleven years old."

"Speaking of Phillip," Rodney said. "You realize we're playing his team next week, right?"

Liam choked on his milk.

"I don't think he realized," Sean said, pounding on Liam's back.

Knowing that he'd be playing Phillip's team in less than a week, Liam threw himself into practices as never before. He spent extra time in the backyard, too, hitting balls his mother or father pitched. And every night after dinner, he updated Carter on his progress.

"I hit three over our fence today," he reported one night. "Serious blasts that I think would have been homers in a game."

"Awesome!"

And after a practice—"I got to play catcher for the first time today. I think Scott might be having second thoughts about Robert."

"Of course he is. Why would he want a lunkhead like Hall when he could have a doofus like you?"

And the night before the game—"I think I'm going to puke I'm so nervous. What if I screw up tomorrow? What if he plays with my mind—"

"What mind?"

"—or gets all up in my grill?"

"You can't pull off that kind of talk, so don't even try."

"Carter?"

"What?"

"What if he strikes me out again?"

Carter leaned in so close nothing but his eyes filled the screen. "He. Won't." Then he sat back. "Now go to bed."

"It's only seven o'clock here."

"Right. Well, it's ten here. So I'm going to bed. Luck." Carter held up his left fist and Liam tapped his screen with his right.

The game was scheduled for three o'clock. Before they left, his mother gripped his shoulders and looked him in the eye.

"It's not going to be easy, facing that boy today."

He lifted his chin. "I know. But I'll be okay. Come on. Let's go."

The Rattlers were the home team, so the Pythons warmed up in the field first. Liam had been assigned to center field, with Rodney and Jay Mendoza at left and right. Rodney started with the ball and threw to Liam. Liam caught it and spun to face Jay. He was about to throw when a movement caught his eye. He froze.

Phillip DiMaggio was walking toward his team's dugout.

"Hello, Earth to Liam!" Jay yelled. "Come on, McGrath, throw it already!"

Phillip stopped abruptly. His head snapped around. His eyes skipped over Jay and landed on Liam.

They stared at each other, neither moving.

Then Phillip slowly lifted a finger, touched his chest, touched his nose, and pointed at Liam.

"Is that—? Are you okay?"

Rodney's voice beside him pulled Liam back.

"I think I need to practice your dad's breathing techniques more," Liam said shakily. Then he threw to Jay.

Ten minutes later, the Rattlers took the field and soon after, the game began.

The Pythons had first raps. Liam watched Phillip take the mound and rifle in some practice throws. His arm looked as strong and his aim as accurate as it had in Williamsport.

Robert was watching Phillip, too. "That's the guy I should be catching for," he muttered. "We'd make a great team, just like he and my brother did."

Liam glanced around at his teammates, wondering if anyone else had heard the comment. Scott was frowning, but Liam wasn't sure if it was because of what Robert said or not.

Finally, the game started.

First baseman Reggie Zimmer grabbed a bat and strode to the plate. Four pitches later, he walked back with a dazed look, having struck out.

"Man, those pitches came fast," he said, reminding Liam that he was just starting out in the Majors.

Alex Kroft, a tall, skinny kid with a pointed nose, moved to the box. He laced a line drive toward third, a surefire single—except that the third baseman somehow caught it.

Now it was Robert's turn. He let the first two go by, swung at the third, and then watched the next two sail wide of the strike zone.

"Take your base!" the umpire called.

Robert tossed his bat aside and trotted to first. Once there, he pounded his hands together and yelled, "Come on, Scott, bring me home!"

The bench took up the call as Scott got into his stance. One pitch went by. Two. Then—

Crack! A sharply hit fly ball jolted Liam and his teammates to their feet.

"It's going, it's going, it's—GONE!" Sean bellowed.

Liam applauded as first Robert and then Scott

touched home plate. But his eyes were on Phillip the whole time. The pitcher was stabbing at the rubber with his toe, clearly disgusted with himself.

Well, what do you know? Liam thought. *Guess there are some kids who can hit off you after all, huh, DiMaggio? And guess who's going to be one of them? Me!*

CHAPTER
TWENTY-SEVEN

Carter held up his glove and waited for Jerry Tuckerman to send him the ball. They and their Hawk teammates were at the Diamond Champs for their first practice. But Jerry seemed more interested in telling Ash about Liam than warming up.

"You should have been there, Ash. *Boom!* That was the sound his bat made when he belted the RBI triple that got us into the U.S. Championship last year." Jerry shook his head. "Doesn't it feel weird to be playing without him, Carter?"

"Yeah," Carter agreed—although *weird* didn't begin to describe how he felt.

He and Liam had been on teams together since they

were four years old. They'd learned the game side by side. They'd celebrated their victories and consoled each other when they lost. Starting the new season without Liam just felt wrong—and at that moment, Carter missed him a lot.

But he couldn't say that to his teammates, so he simply repeated, "Yeah, Jerry, it does feel weird."

"I'll tell you what's weird," Ash said, "the fact that you still haven't thrown the ball, Tuckerman!"

"Huddle up, Hawks, huddle up, huddle up!"

The call came from their coach, Mr. Harrison. Carter, Jerry, and Ash hustled to the bench with their teammates.

When Carter had received his team assignment last week, he'd been psyched to see that he had Mr. Harrison for a coach again. He'd also been happy to see Jerry, Miguel, Leo, Remy, and Ash on the Hawks roster. He didn't recognize all of the other names, but he figured he'd get to know his other teammates soon enough.

"Today's practice starts with a half hour, six-on-six infield-only scrimmage," the coach announced. "Then we have time in the cages. So let's make the most of it, yes?"

He consulted his clipboard. "Scrimmage positions are as follows. Carter, pitcher! Ash, catcher! Jerry, Kevin, Miguel, Leo—first, second, short, and third! The rest of you are batting in this order: Josh, Jared, Remy, Arthur, Seth, and Drew. Understood? Okay! Hands in the middle now. One, two, three—"

"—*Hawks*!"

Carter hurried to the mound. Ash jogged to the plate. Their assistant coach, Mr. Walker, acted as umpire. Carter threw a few final warm-up pitches and then Coach Walker yelled, "Batter up!"

Josh Samuels, an eleven-year-old with a mop of hair tucked under his cap, looked about as likely to get a hit as Carter's dog. Carter had never played with him before, so he didn't know what he was capable of. He decided it was better not to underestimate him.

He leaned in and stared down at the plate. Ash flashed the signal for a fastball low and inside. Carter nodded once. Then he straightened, went into his windup, and threw.

The ball sizzled on a line straight from Carter's hand—*thud!*—to Ash's glove. Josh didn't even try for it.

"Strike!" Coach Walker cried.

Ash threw the ball back to Carter. "That-a-boy, Jones, that-a-boy!" he called, thumping his fist into his mitt. "Let's see it again, rifle it right past him, you can do it!"

Carter blinked. In all the time they had been

practicing together, Ash had never let loose with such a stream of chatter. Carter wished he could tell him to stop. But instead, he just waited for his catcher to get back into his crouch.

This time, Ash signaled for a changeup. Again, Carter threw—and again, Josh stood like a statue.

"Strike two!"

That cry was followed by another enthusiastic outburst from Ash. This time, the other Hawks in the field joined in, their voices echoing off the walls. Carter closed his eyes, trying to block out the noise. He hoped one of the coaches would tell them to pipe down. But Mr. Harrison was busy showing one of the other batters a good grip on the bat, while Mr. Walker readied himself for the next pitch.

The chatter seemed to wake up Josh, for he swung at the third pitch, another fastball. But he missed for strike three and the first out.

The next two batters, Jared Levy and Remy Werner, weren't any more trouble than Josh was. Carter retired the side without giving up a hit.

Back on the bench, Carter sat down next to Ash. "Listen," he started to say.

But Ash cut him off. "Watch out for Arthur in the

next inning. He's been coming to the batting cages a lot. He's got a good eye." Then Ash turned his attention to the game. "Start us off, Miguel!"

Miguel Martinez stepped into the box. He let Drew Meeker's first pitch go by but clocked the second one for a bouncing grounder between short and third. Jerry got a hit, too, putting runners on first and second. Leo looked eager to keep things rolling, but instead lined out to first. Unfortunately, Jerry had taken too big a lead. All Arthur Holmes had to do was step on the bag for the double play.

Now Ash came up to bat. Carter had seen him connect over and over with balls hurled from a pitching machine. He hoped Ash could do as well off a live pitcher.

He could. *Crack!* In fact, Ash hit the ball so hard it caromed off the wall behind center field! As he passed his squad's bench, he called, "How'd you like that *boom*, Jerry?"

Miguel scored, and Ash landed on second. That was the only run scored their turn at bat, however, for second baseman Kevin Pinto flied out.

As the two groups switched sides, Carter finally had a chance to ask Ash to ease up on the chatter. "It's just really distracting," he said apologetically. "So can you maybe save it for when we're outside?"

Ash shrugged. "Gee, I dunno. Sure seemed to help last inning. Now head to the mound—and remember what I told you about Arthur."

CHAPTER
TWENTY-EIGHT

Woo-hoo! Two runs on the board, baby!" Rodney cheered as he jogged to the plate. "Time to make it three!"

Liam and the other Pythons cheered, too. But their cries died when Rodney struck out to end the top of the first inning. Liam grabbed his glove and hurried to his spot in center field. He passed DiMaggio on the way and the two locked eyes for a long moment. Rodney must have seen the exchange, for when he and Liam were in position, he yelled a piece of advice to Liam.

"Breathe!" he called from left field.

Liam took that advice while Scott threw some warm-up pitches. To his surprise, the deep inhalations and exhalations actually seemed to help. When the bottom of the first inning began, he felt calmer and more focused.

I'll have to tell Carter to give it a try!

Thinking of his cousin brought a sudden lump to his throat. Rodney, Sean, and the others all knew about Liam's history with Phillip. But only Carter really understood, because only Carter knew Liam inside and out.

Plus, he realized with a start, *Carter had been humiliated by Phillip, too.* He'd been so busy worrying about his own problems he'd completely forgotten his cousin's troubles with DiMaggio at baseball camp.

You owe Carter a jersey, he thought fiercely. *And somehow, some day I'll make sure you pay up!*

With that, he turned his attention to the game.

Scott mowed down the first batter on three straight pitches. The next Rattler gave him a little more trouble, fouling the ball four times. All were grounders, making them impossible to catch for an out.

On the fifth pitch, however—*tick!*—the batter popped up the ball in front of the plate. It should have been an easy out for Robert to make. But he struggled to get his mask off and the ball fell in the dirt. While he scrambled to pick it up, the runner sprinted safely to first.

"Play is to first or second!" Liam yelled from center field. "Let's try for two to end this inning!"

The third batter pinged a bouncing ground ball that looked as if it leaped into Alex Kroft's glove on purpose. The third baseman zipped it to Sean at second. The runner was out—and so was the batter, for Sean's throw beat him to first.

"Yes!" Liam cried, slapping Sean's palm when he reached the dugout. Then he selected a bat and waited for his turn at the plate. He was up after the inning's leadoff hitter, shortstop Clint Kelley. He cheered for Clint with his teammates, but kept his eye on Phillip, studying his mechanics so he'd be ready to face him.

He didn't get to see many pitches, however, for the Pythons shortstop rapped out a single on the second pitch.

Liam headed to the plate. Before he reached the box, he glanced at the assistant coach. Mr. Dumas gave the signal for a bunt.

Liam felt a curl of disappointment. He wanted to try teeing off on Phillip—badly. But he knew the bunt made more sense.

"Li-am. Li-am. Li-am." A single voice in the stands started the chant.

He rolled his eyes. He knew whom the voice belonged

to without even looking. *Melanie*, he thought. *Man, she'll do anything for attention!*

But secretly, he was pleased his sister was there for him.

He straightened his batting helmet, stepped into the box, hefted the bat over his shoulder, and faced DiMaggio.

They locked eyes for a long moment. The pitcher gave a half smile. Liam wished he could knock that look right off his face. But he knew better than to disregard his coach's instructions.

Next time, DiMaggio, he vowed.

The pitch came. Liam squared off and poked the ball straight down. As it dribbled down the third-base line, he took off for first. For one fleeting moment, he thought he could beat the throw. But he didn't.

"Out!"

Well, at least I moved Clint to second, he thought as he circled back to the dugout. Unfortunately, Clint died on base when Sean and Jay both struck out.

The Rattlers didn't earn any runs their turn at bat either. Neither did the Pythons. But in the bottom of the third, the Rattlers got on the board thanks to a sizzling RBI double off Phillip's bat.

Liam got up to bat again in the top of the fourth

inning. This time, he got to swing away. He connected, too—for three foul balls in a row. He straightened out the fourth, but it was a weak shot the third baseman had no trouble handling. His out ended their chances to score that inning.

He felt Phillip's eyes mocking him the whole way to the dugout. But he refused to get rattled.

Channel your anger, he told himself, *and get him next time.*

But there was no next time. While the Rattlers nearly tied the game in the fourth inning when Jay bobbled a catch in right field, the next three batters made outs and the runner died on base. The Pythons were blanked their last two at bats, as were the Rattlers in the bottom of the fifth.

By the bottom of the sixth inning, the score was still Pythons 2, Rattlers 1.

The Rattlers were at the top of their order. On the mound, Scott was flagging. He got the first batter out, but gave up singles to the next two.

With runners on first and second, the Rattlers big hitter, Phillip DiMaggio, was in the batter's box.

Liam expected Robert to wave the outfielders back. It was the catcher's job to direct the play on the field, after all, and Robert had to know that Scott was tiring and Phillip had a good chance of creaming the ball.

But Robert just got into his crouch.

Idiot, Liam thought. Then he called to his fellow outfielders to move back. It was a good thing he did because—*Crack!*—Phillip connected on Scott's first pitch, a massive blast that soared high in the sky between center and left field!

Liam and Rodney both took off after it.

"I've got it!" Liam bellowed.

Rodney backed off immediately. Liam churned up the grass, eyes glued to the ball. As it started to drop, he put on a burst of speed. Then, his heart hammering in his chest and his arm stretching as far as he could reach, he dove across the turf—and slid his glove under the ball just before it hit the ground!

Phillip was out! But the play wasn't over yet. Liam leaped to his feet and spotted the runners returning to their bases. Shortstop Clint Kelley was in the cutoff position. But there wasn't time for the relay.

"Duck!" Liam shouted to Clint.

Clint ducked. Liam heaved the ball to Sean at second. It was a perfect throw that socked into Sean's glove with a loud pop. Sean swept it down seconds before the runner tagged up.

For a split second, there was dead silence. Then—

"Yer out!" the umpire yelled.

Sean gave a whoop. Jay and Rodney converged on Liam, slapping him on the back as they ran in from the outfield. In the stands, Melanie and the McGraths cheered loud and long, almost to the point of embarrassment. Coach Dumas gave him a high five that left Liam's palm stinging while Coach Driscoll nodded and said, "Well done."

Final score: Pythons 2, Rattlers 1.

After the game, the teams lined up for the traditional hand-slap. As he began to move, Liam felt a jolt of adrenaline surge through his veins. Every step was bringing him closer to Phillip.

And then, they were face-to-face. Time slowed as they regarded each other.

"Good game, DiMaggio," Liam finally said. He raised his palm a little higher.

Phillip looked at it. Then he narrowed his eyes, touched his hand to Liam's, and said, "Until next time, McGrath."

CHAPTER
TWENTY-NINE

Come on, Jones, put it in here! Put it in here! Put it in here!"

Carter couldn't believe his ears when Ash let out another string of chatter.

It's like he didn't even hear me! he thought.

He picked up the ball and threw it into his glove as hard as he could. Once, twice, three times, all while staring hard at the catcher. But either Ash didn't see his look or didn't care because he just kept talking.

First up was Arthur Holmes. Carter and Arthur had a few classes together at school, and while Arthur never said much, Carter got the impression he was very smart.

He certainly was smart about the pitches he swung

at. Carter's first throw, a changeup, dipped a little too soon. Arthur didn't even try for it.

"Ball one!" Mr. Walker called.

Arthur let the second sinker go by as well for ball two.

Time for something different, Carter thought. So when Ash signaled for a third changeup, he shook him off.

Ash frowned and flashed the same signal again. Again, Carter shook it off and waited for Ash to give him something else.

Instead, Ash spread his hands as if to say, *go ahead, it's your call.*

So Carter threw a two-seam fastball.

Pow! Arthur connected for a screaming line drive between second and short. Carter spun around in time to see Miguel and Kevin dive for the catch. Both missed, but nearly hit each other.

From the sidelines, Coach Harrison instructed Arthur to hold up at second while Leo retrieved the ball.

"Hey, what gives?"

Carter whirled around to find Ash standing behind him, glaring.

"I told you to be careful with him," Ash said.

"I—sorry," Carter stammered, taken aback. "I thought I could get him with the fastball."

"Yeah? Well, you thought wrong. Next time, don't shake me off. I know what I'm doing."

He stalked back to the plate and got into his crouch. Carter wondered if he'd start up the chatter again. But this time, the catcher stayed silent. And somehow, that was worse than the noise.

Seth Wynne came up to bat. He topped the first pitch, sending it straight down in front of the plate. Ash was up on his feet like a shot. He whipped his mask off, scooped up the ball with his bare hand, checked Arthur at second, and then threw to first. Seth was out—and Jerry was pulling his hand out of his glove and shaking it.

"Yeouch!" he cried. "That was a bullet, Ash!"

"There's plenty more where that came from!" Ash replied, drawing laughter from the other Hawks.

Carter laughed, too, although he couldn't help wondering why Ash had thrown so hard when it was clear he could get Seth out.

The next two batters, Drew and Josh, both struck out. Mr. Harrison gave them a few words of encouragement as they collected their gloves, then pointed to Carter.

"Okay, Jones, let's see what you've got at the plate this year!"

195

Carter nodded and hustled to the batter's box. He'd been concentrating so much on pitching in the last weeks that he hadn't done much hitting. Fortunately, Drew gave him a pitch he liked. He connected solidly for a turf-buzzing grounder in the gap between first and second.

"Give me a ticket home!" he called to Miguel.

Miguel grounded out. But Jerry pounded Drew's third pitch far into right field, reaching second and sending Carter to third. Leo lined out to the pitcher. Drew looked so surprised to see the ball back in his glove, Carter almost laughed out loud.

Now Ash came up to bat. His last hit had flown beyond anyone's reach. The players hushed as they waited to see what he would do this time. Mr. Harrison leaned forward, hands on knees, watching Ash intently.

Drew threw. Ash swung and missed.

Drew hurled a second pitch. Ash let it go by.

"Strike!"

Carter licked his lips nervously, wondering if Ash was going to choke with the runners in scoring position.

He got his answer two pitches later. The first was wide. The second was right on the money. Ash took another huge cut—and went down swinging.

Carter and his teammates jogged in. Carter started to reassure Ash that it didn't matter, it was just a practice.

"Just get out there and pitch," Ash cut him off with a snarl. "And this time, don't shake me off."

Stunned, Carter picked up his glove and moved to the mound. *He's just embarrassed,* he told himself.

Jared Levy came to the plate. Ash signaled for a fastball. Carter nodded, reared back, and threw. Jared swung from the heels and missed.

Ash returned the ball to Carter and called for the same pitch. Jared missed that one, too.

Carter thought Ash would change things then. Instead, he flashed the same fingers again. This time, Jared connected for a single.

Remy stepped into the batter's box. Carter looked in and Ash showed three fingers.

A changeup. Carter shifted his grip, wound up, and threw. Remy fanned.

Three fingers again.

Carter frowned.

Another changeup? Is he testing me or something? Daring me to question him?

If so, Carter didn't feel like playing that game. He delivered the pitch Ash signaled for.

Remy fouled the ball down the third-base line.

When Ash signaled for yet another changeup, Carter didn't hesitate to throw it even though he was sure Remy would see it coming.

Remy did. His bat met the ball and sent it bouncing past Leo at third.

Runners at first and second, and now Arthur Holmes was up at bat. Carter leaned in.

What're you going to give me this time, Ash?

When the signal came, he blinked, not sure he'd seen it right. Ash flashed it again. There was no mistaking it this time.

Curveball, those fingers said.

Now Carter knew for sure: Ash was testing him, all right. Big time.

After the pitching tryouts, Carter had told Ash everything Coach Harrison had said about the curveball. He also told him that if he was put on Mr. Harrison's team, he wouldn't throw the pitch or practice it.

Ash had immediately urged him to rethink his decision. "I'm not saying you use it all the time. But come on, what's the harm in practicing it now and then? That way, it's ready when you need it!"

"But Coach Harrison—"

"—said it wasn't against the rules," Ash finished flatly.

"What's the holdup, Carter?" the coach called. "We're running out of time!"

Carter glanced at the coach and nodded. Then he rotated the ball in his hand, took a deep breath, reared back, and threw.

CHAPTER
THIRTY

"And after the high five, he says, 'Until next time, McGrath!' all menacing and threatening-like," Liam finished gleefully.

Liam had arrived home an hour ago, still jazzed from the win over the Rattlers. The Driscolls had invited him for pizza, but he had declined. "Got a call to make," he said.

When he got home, he immediately Skyped Carter, knowing his cousin wouldn't go to bed until he'd heard the details.

Carter grinned. "Who cares what he said? You made the play that stopped him cold!"

"Yeah. I just wish I'd gotten a monster hit off him. That would have been sweet."

"There's still time. Lots of games to come, right?"

"Right. And hopefully, I'll be behind the plate for at least some of them."

"How'd that kid Robert do?"

"Worse than lousy, plus his attitude stinks." Liam leaned back and laced his fingers behind his head. "Unless he improves really quickly, I think I could be wearing the mask and pads again real soon."

"That's where you should be."

Liam gave a short laugh. "Actually, where I should be is back in Pennsylvania. But since I can't be, I'll take playing catcher." He sat forward. "But enough about me. You had your first practice today, right? How'd it go? Was that indoor field any good? What'd you do for drills? Did you get to pitch? And who caught for you?"

Carter shrugged. "Practice went okay. Coach Harrison is great, of course, and I think we've got some decent players, so hopefully we'll have a good season." He gave a tremendous yawn then. "Listen, Liam, I gotta get to bed. But I'm psyched for you, man, I really am."

He lifted his fist to the screen. Liam touched his

own knuckles to it three times and then the cousins signed off.

It wasn't until the screen went blank that Liam realized Carter never said who his new catcher was.

Oh well, he thought, *I'm sure I'll find out soon enough.*

Back in Pennsylvania, Carter pulled the covers up to his chin. But as tired as he was, he couldn't fall asleep. Part of the trouble, he knew, was that he'd avoided answering Liam's questions about his catcher. The other part was the reason he'd avoided answering: the catcher himself.

Weeks ago, Carter couldn't imagine anyone taking Liam's place behind the plate. Slowly, though, he'd gotten used to the idea of seeing Ash there. But after this evening's practice, he wasn't so sure anymore.

When he threw a two-seam fastball instead of the curve the catcher had signaled for, Carter had figured Ash wouldn't be happy with him. And he wasn't wrong. Ash had given him the cold shoulder the rest of practice. The ride home would have been silent if not for Mrs. LaBrie's chatter.

It's that darned curveball! Carter thought now. *I wish I'd never tried it. I mean, sure, I can get it over the plate. But just because I can throw it doesn't mean I should—or ever will! I've got to make sure he understands I'm not throwing it again.*

He looked out his window toward the McGraths' house. It was late, but he could see a light on in Liam's bedroom.

The LaBries' house, he amended. *Ash's bedroom.*

He found his phone and sent Ash a short text. *How about a catch tomorrow after breakfast?* it read.

He waited for a reply, but didn't get one. Then the light in Ash's bedroom went out. Knowing there was nothing more he could do that night, Carter finally drifted off to sleep.

Sunday morning, Carter woke to the buzz of his cell phone. Ash had replied to his text.

Your yard or mine? it read.

Carter breathed a sigh of relief. *At least we're talking again,* he thought as he typed *Mine in half an hour* and hit send.

Exactly half an hour later, Ash appeared at the Joneses' door. With Lucky Boy in tow, the boys headed to Carter's backyard and began tossing the ball to each other. For a few minutes, the only sounds were the smack of the ball hitting their gloves and Lucky Boy's excited yips as he dashed between them.

"Listen, Ash," Carter finally said, "I'm done with the curveball, okay? I've got plenty of other pitches I can use."

"Sure you do," Ash said agreeably. "They're good pitches, too. But so is your curve." When Carter started to protest, Ash held up his hand. "I'm not saying you'll ever use it. But why not practice it from time to time, just in case you need it someday?"

"I'll never need it."

Ash raised his eyebrows. "Really? Never? How about if you were on the mound for the final inning of the U.S. Championship Game with the score tied—and Phillip DiMaggio came up to bat?"

Carter snorted in disbelief. "The odds of DiMaggio and me meeting at Williamsport again are like a gazillion to one, Ash, you know that! I mean, when's the last time the same two Little League teams reached the World Series tournament? And even if both our teams did get that far, the chance of us meeting in the U.S. Championship Game? Forget it!"

Ash waved his protests away impatiently. "You didn't answer my question. If you could win the U.S. Championship and advance to the World Series match by throwing it, would you?" He narrowed his eyes. "Would you use it to strike out DiMaggio the way he struck out your cousin?"

Images of DiMaggio swinging and missing, of Liam leaping and pumping his fists in triumph, of teammates swarming him on the mound, flashed with sudden clarity in Carter's mind—and for one long moment, he could see himself using the curveball just that once.

Then he came back to reality. He tossed the ball in the air and then started throwing it hard into his glove. Over and over, it struck the pocket with a solid thud. When he finally answered Ash, his voice was firm.

"Like I said, there's zero chance of me throwing any kind of pitch to DiMaggio again. So let's just drop the whole curveball thing and get on with playing catch, okay?"

Ash scowled and kicked at the grass. "All right, fine." Then he fixed Carter with an intense gaze. "I just have one last question."

Carter stiffened. "What?" he asked warily.

"Do you still want to go all the way to Williamsport this year?"

" 'Course I do!" Carter replied, tossing the ball back to him. "And I know just how to get there."

"Yeah? How?"

Carter smiled. "One step at a time."

A LITTLE LEAGUE BOOK

WHAT IS LITTLE LEAGUE®?

With nearly 165,000 teams in all 50 states and over 80 other countries across the globe, Little League Baseball® is the world's largest organized youth sports program! Many of today's Major League players started their baseball careers in Little League Baseball, including Derek Jeter, David Wright, Justin Verlander, and Adrian Gonzalez.

Little League® is a nonprofit organization that works to teach the principles of sportsmanship, fair play, and teamwork. Concentrating on discipline, character, and courage, Little League is focused on more than just developing athletes: It helps to create upstanding citizens.

Carl Stotz established Little League in 1939 in Williamsport, Pennsylvania. The first league only had three teams and played six innings, but by 1946, there were already twelve leagues throughout the state of Pennsylvania. The following year, 1947, was the first year that the Little League Baseball® World Series was played, and it has continued to be played every August since then.

In 1951, Little League Baseball expanded internationally, and the first permanent league to form outside of the United States was on each end of the Panama Canal. Little League Baseball later moved to nearby South Williamsport, Pennsylvania, and a second stadium, the Little League Volunteer Stadium, was opened in 2001.

Some key moments in Little League history:

- **1957** The Monterrey, Mexico, team became the first international team to win the World Series.
- **1964** Little League was granted a federal charter.
- **1974** The federal charter was amended to allow girls to join Little League.
- **1982** The Peter J. McGovern Little League Museum opened.
- **1989** Little League introduced the Challenger Division.
- **2001** The World Series expanded from eight to sixteen teams to provide a greater opportunity for children to participate in the World Series.
- **2014** Little League will celebrate its 75th anniversary.

HOW DOES A LITTLE LEAGUE® TEAM GET TO THE WORLD SERIES?

In order to play in the Little League Baseball World Series, a player must first be a part of a regular-season Little League, and then be selected as part of their league's All-Star team, consisting of players ages 11 to 13 from any of the teams. The All-Star teams compete in district, sectional, and state tournaments to become their state champions. The state champions then compete to represent one of eight different geographic regions of the United States (New England, Mid-Atlantic, Southeast, Great Lakes, Midwest, Northwest, Southwest, and West). All eight of the Regional Tournament winners play in the Little League Baseball World Series.

The eight International Tournament winners (representing Asia-Pacific and the Middle East, Australia, Canada, the Caribbean, Europe and Africa, Mexico, Japan, and Latin America) also come to the Little League Baseball World Series.

The eight U.S. Regional Tournament winners compete in the United States Bracket of the Little League

Baseball World Series, and the International Tournament winners compete in the International Bracket.

Over eleven days, the Little League Baseball World Series proceeds until a winning U.S. Championship team and International Championship team are determined. The final World Series Championship Game is played between the U.S. Champions and the International Champions.

WANT TO LEARN MORE?

Visit the Peter J. McGovern Little League Museum in South Williamsport, Pennsylvania! When you visit, you'll find pictures, displays, films, and exhibits showcasing the history of Little League, from the players all the way down to the equipment. A renovated museum opened in summer 2013.

BATTER UP!
A LITTLE LEAGUE® POP QUIZ!

You think that you know all there is to know about Little League? Now is your chance to prove it! Take the quiz below to test your Little League knowledge.

1. When was Little League Baseball founded?
   a. 1914
   b. 1925
   c. 1939
   d. 1941

2. When did the first Little League Baseball World Series occur?
   a. 1940
   b. 1947
   c. 1949
   d. 1953

3. Where was Little League Baseball founded?
   a. Williamsport, PA
   b. Bloomsburg, PA
   c. Lock Haven, PA
   d. Hammonton, NJ

4. Which of the following is not a region represented in the Little League Baseball World Series?
   a. Midwest   c. North
   b. Southeast   d. West

5. Where was the first permanent international Little League formed?
   a. Mexico   c. Japan
   b. Canada   d. Panama

6. How many innings are in a Little League Baseball game?
   a. 3   c. 6
   b. 5   d. 9

7. In which month of the year is the annual Little League Baseball World Series held?
   a. March   c. July
   b. May   d. August

8. How many teams participate in Little League Baseball?
   a. 8   c. 200
   b. 16   d. almost 165,000

If you answer all of the questions correctly, you get a Grand Slam!

If you answer seven or more of the questions correctly, you get a Home Run.

Five correct answers give you a Triple, three bring you to Second Base, and one gets you on First.

If you don't answer any of the questions correctly, then you've Struck Out. In that case, it's time to read more about Little League Baseball!

HOW CAN I JOIN A
LITTLE LEAGUE® TEAM?

If you have access to the Internet, you can see if your community has a local league by going to www.LittleLeague.org and clicking on "Start/Find a League." You can also visit one of our regional offices:

US REGIONAL OFFICES:
Western Region Headquarters (AK, AZ, CA, HI, ID, MT, NV, OR, UT, WA, and WY)
6707 Little League Drive
San Bernardino, CA 92407
E-MAIL: westregion@LittleLeague.org

Southwestern Region Headquarters (AR, CO, LA, MS, NM, OK, and TX)
3700 South University Parks Drive
Waco, TX 76706
E-MAIL: southwestregion@LittleLeague.org

Central Region Headquarters (IA, IL, IN, KS, KY, MI, MN, MO, ND, NE, OH, SD, and WI)
9802 E. Little League Drive
Indianapolis, IN 46235
E-MAIL: centralregion@LittleLeague.org

Southeastern Region Headquarters (AL, FL, GA, NC, SC, TN, VA, and WV)
PO Box 7557
Warner Robins, GA 31095
E-MAIL: southeastregion@LittleLeague.org

Eastern Region Headquarters (CT, DC, DE, MD, ME, NH, NJ, NY, PA, RI, and VT)
PO Box 2926
Bristol, CT 06011
E-MAIL: eastregion@LittleLeague.org

INTERNATIONAL REGIONAL OFFICES:
CANADIAN REGION (serving all of Canada)
Canadian Little League Headquarters
235 Dale Avenue
Ottawa, ONT
Canada KIG OH6
E-MAIL: Canada@LittleLeague.org

ASIA-PACIFIC REGION (serving all of Asia and Australia)
Asia-Pacific Regional Director
C/O Hong Kong Little League
Room 1005, Sports House
1 Stadium Path
Causeway Bay, Hong Kong
E-MAIL: bhc368@netvigator.com

EUROPE, MIDDLE EAST & AFRICA REGION
(serving all of Europe, the Middle East, and Africa)
Little League Europe
A1. Meleg Legi 1
Kutno, 99-300, Poland
E-MAIL: Europe@LittleLeague.org

LATIN AMERICA REGION (serving Mexico and Latin American regions)
Latin America Little League Headquarters
PO Box 10237
Caparra Heights, Puerto Rico 00922-0237
E-MAIL: LatinAmerica@LittleLeague.org

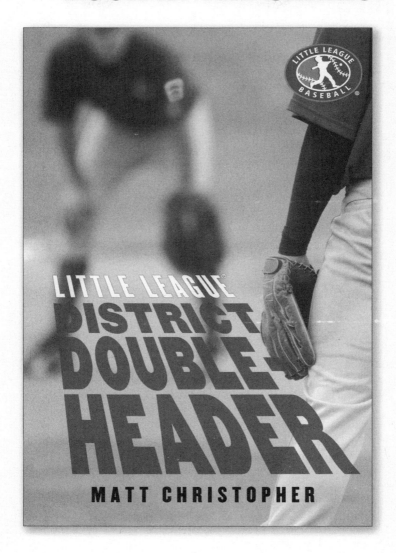

CHAPTER ONE

"Look who's here."

Liam McGrath, starting catcher for the Pythons in their game against the Cobras, glanced sideways at his teammate Rodney Driscoll. Rodney ran his hand over his tight black curls and then jerked his chin toward the bleachers. Liam looked over and his mouth tightened.

"Phillip DiMaggio," he muttered. "Great. What's he doing here?"

Rodney shrugged. "Taking in a game? Checking out the competition? Trying to decide who to vote for as an All-Star?"

Liam flinched at the mention of the vote. He'd been an All-Star last year and wanted to be one again this year.

But he didn't think that was likely. Last year he'd been a leader, a player teammates turned to when the pressure was on. Now he was the new kid in town, an unknown. Or worse, known for something he wished no one knew.

He twisted his Pythons baseball cap around so the brim covered his neck and pulled his catcher's helmet into place over his face and throat guard.

He knew he shouldn't be surprised to see Phillip. After all, they lived in the same town now. Played in the same local Little League, too, although for different teams, thankfully. If he had been assigned to DiMaggio's team, he didn't know what he would have done.

Yes, I do. I would have played, he thought, *because I'm not a quitter.* But it wouldn't have been easy seeing his nemesis at practices every week, and having to cheer him on during games, and maybe even—Liam gulped at the thought—catching for him.

Liam and Phillip had first met the previous August at the Little League Baseball World Series in Williamsport, Pennsylvania. At that time, Liam was still living in Pennsylvania, close to his cousin and best friend, Carter Jones. That summer, he, Carter, and their All-Star teammates had accomplished an amazing feat: They had beaten all the other teams from the Mid-Atlantic Region to earn a berth at the World Series. They had won the majority of their games in the World Series tournament, too, and advanced to the U.S. Championship.

Their opponent in that game was a Southern California team representing the West Region. The West's pitcher was Phillip DiMaggio.

Liam had no clue who DiMaggio was then, but Carter did. He'd had a run-in with the pitcher during Little League Baseball Camp the summer before. And two days before the United States Championship, Carter told Liam all about it.

"Because of his last name, I thought he was related to the great Joe DiMaggio." Carter scrubbed his hands over his face. "So I asked him to autograph my camp jersey. But of course, I had forgotten Joltin' Joe doesn't have any direct heirs. Phillip called me Number One Fan the rest of camp—he thought it was hysterical. I thought it was humiliating."

When Carter told him the story, Liam didn't get mad. In fact, he said it probably helped Carter to use his anger at Phillip as motivation to become a better pitcher. Still, he didn't like the trick Phillip had pulled. The first time Liam came face-to-face with DiMaggio, Liam played a prank of his own. He poked a spot on the pitcher's shirt and told him he had a stain. When Phillip looked down, Liam jerked his finger up, bopped Phillip in the nose, and chortled, "Made you look!"

That innocent prank came back to haunt him during the U.S. Championship Game.

Mid-Atlantic was down a run in the bottom of the sixth. Phillip was on the mound. Liam came up to bat. There was a runner on third, two outs. Liam let the first pitch go by for a called strike. He nicked the second for a foul and strike two. Determined to hit a game-winning homer off DiMaggio, he took a monstrous swing at the third pitch—and missed.

Worse than missed. He swung so hard that he corkscrewed around off-balance and fell face-first into the dirt. In front of thousands of spectators. On live television.

Game over.

Moments later, Phillip offered him a hand to help him up. To the viewers watching at home, the gesture looked like the epitome of sportsmanship. But the cameras and microphones missed something. With a flick of his outstretched finger, Phillip brushed Liam's shirt and then touched the batter's nose.

"Hey, McGrath," he whispered, pointing at Liam. "Made you whiff!"

Back home, Liam had tried to remember everything good that had happened during the World Series and to put that one bad moment behind him. But that was easier said than done. First, he discovered that a video clip of his strikeout was available for viewing by anyone who had access to the Internet. Second, he learned that his family was moving across the country to Southern California. Third, and most unbelievable, he found out that he would now be living in the same town as Phillip DiMaggio.

Liam risked another glance at the stands. He panned over the spectators—an older man with a stern expression and almond-shaped eyes, a pair of girls giggling together, a group of parents—then landed on Phillip. His brown eyes met the pitcher's jet-black ones for a brief moment. Then Phillip looked away.

Liam adjusted his leg guards and hurried out onto the field.

He'd survived moving across the country, leaving all his friends. If he'd been put on the same team as DiMaggio, he would have survived that, too. No, better than survived. He would have succeeded.

Last August, it was game over, he thought. *From here on out, it's game on.*

CHAPTER TWO

Carter Jones bagged the pile of leaves he'd been raking and carried it to the parking lot. It was Little League Cleanup Day, and along with dozens of other players, parents, and Little League coaches, he was getting the baseball fields ready for the upcoming season.

"Hustle over, everyone. Team meeting!" Mr. Harrison, coach of the Hawks, called. A wiry man with thick black hair, he had been Carter and Liam's coach last year and throughout the All-Star team's run in the postseason. Carter counted himself very lucky to have been drafted to his team again this time around. It took some of the sting out of being separated from Liam.

Some, but not all. Until Liam moved, he and Carter

were inseparable. They were the same age, had the same friends, and went to the same school. They slept at each other's houses, shared meals, and celebrated every birthday and holiday together.

They played baseball together, too, and were teammates from Little League Tee Ball all the way up through the Major Division. When Carter began pitching regularly on their Majors team, Liam became his catcher. They proved to be a formidable duo on the field.

"It's like you can read each other's minds," a fellow player once marveled.

Carter thought that wasn't far from the truth. Maybe he and Liam didn't have an actual psychic link like in science-fiction books, but they did share a connection that was stronger than most. And now that the Little League season was about to begin, Carter missed his cousin more than ever.

In the dugout, a blond-haired boy named Ash La-Brie waved Carter over. "Got room here."

Carter hesitated before taking the seat. He liked Ash but felt disloyal to Liam whenever he hung out with him. For one thing, Ash and his mother had moved into Liam's old house. Now Ash ate in Liam's kitchen, hung out in Liam's living room, and slept in Liam's bedroom. As if that wasn't weird enough, he had also taken over Liam's position as Carter's catcher. Ash was good behind the plate, no doubt, but...well, he wasn't Liam and that was that.

Coach Harrison opened the meeting by thanking them for their hard work. "The concession stand now has a nice new coat of paint. And apparently, so do some of you!"

The players who had been painting looked at their blue-flecked clothing and laughed.

"Hmm," the coach continued, noting a similar smudge of paint on his arm, "guess I should have said 'some of *us*.' And now some more good news. The Hawks are adding a new player to their roster."

He looked toward the parking lot. "Ah, there's your new teammate now!"

He pointed to a person jogging across the field. The kid's cap was shading his face, so it was only when he reached the dugout that everyone realized—

"It's a *girl*!" shortstop Arthur Holmes blurted out.

Carter was surprised, too. He knew Little League Baseball was open to boys and girls; still, actually having a girl on the team was unexpected.

"Everyone, please welcome Rachel Warburton," the coach said. "She just got called up from the Minors."

That's when Carter finally recognized her. They'd been in the same class in fourth grade. Back then, she had worn her long brown hair loose and had a quick, easy grin that invited everyone near her to smile back. Her hair was shorter now and tucked through her cap. But when she saw him, that same grin lit up her face.

"Hey, Carter!" she said. "Got room for me?"

Carter blushed, embarrassed at being singled out, but said, "Uh, sure." He nudged Ash. Ash gave him a look and then slid over.

Rachel sat between them and whispered, "I watched the whole World Series last year. You were awesome!"

Carter reddened even more. "Thanks."

"I was sorry to hear Liam moved away. That must be terrible for—"

"Hey, do you guys mind?" Ash interrupted tersely. "The coach is talking."

Carter immediately snapped his attention back to Mr. Harrison. The coach reminded them they were expected to attend all practices. He also assured them they would each see playing time in every game.

"Finally, remember that win or lose, you support your fellow Hawks and congratulate your opponents. Understood?"

Cheers rose from the kids on the bench.

The meeting ended then. But before Carter could return to his job, the coach called him over. "You too, Ash," he added.

Then he said something that took Carter completely by surprise. "I've been thinking about your curveball."

At Ash's urging, Carter had experimented with that pitch. He thought he was throwing it well, too, and hoped to add it to his pitching arsenal when the season began.

When Coach Harrison found out about it, however, he'd made his disapproval clear. He told Carter that the curve could damage a young pitcher's arm. While Little League didn't outright forbid the pitch, he let Carter know that he certainly didn't want any of his pitchers throwing it. Carter had dropped the curve then and there—much to Ash's displeasure.

"I still don't want you to throw the curveball," the coach said now. "However, I wonder if you'd like some help on your knuckleball instead?"

Carter's green eyes widened. He'd tried the knuckleball before without much success, but he was sure he could master it with Coach Harrison's help. "Absolutely! You tell me when and where, and I'll be there!"

"It won't be me," Mr. Harrison corrected. "A new

volunteer in the league, Mark Delaney, is running a pitching clinic Monday evening at the high school. He needs catchers, too," he added, looking at Ash. "If he likes what he sees, he'll spend time with you on the knuckleball. So, I take it you're interested?"

"Absolutely!" Carter said again.

"Me too," Ash said.

"Me three!"

Carter turned in surprise. He hadn't heard Rachel approach, but there she was, standing behind him and looking at the coach hopefully.

Ash narrowed his eyes. "*You* want to pitch?"

"Heck, I want to try playing anywhere and everywhere," she said, "except 'left out'!"

The joke was completely lame and yet Carter laughed. So did the coach.

"Then you should attend, too," Mr. Harrison said. "Never hurts to have another hurler in the bull pen. Right, boys?"

"Right!" Carter said.

Ash murmured something, too. But whether he was agreeing with the coach, Carter couldn't be sure.